"Too bad your insides aren't as attractive as your outsides," Cameron said, his voice suddenly bitter.

"What's *that* supposed to mean?" Jessica asked.

"You're interested only in people with classy titles or flashy cars or tons of money!"

"And you're a sanctimonious jerk!" Jessica yelled back, jabbing a finger at the mail-room clerk's chest. "You're stuck in a dead-end job so you're jealous of people who have the potential to go higher than that!"

Suddenly Jessica was aware of how close Cameron was standing. If they hadn't been screaming at each other, they could have been slow dancing. Without thinking about it, Jessica tilted her head back to kiss him. For a second Cameron seemed to be leaning forward. Then he scowled and turned away.

"And isn't that just like a model," he observed bitterly. "You all assume that every guy is dying to kiss you, anytime you're ready. Well, this guy isn't! I kiss when *I* choose to. And *only* when I choose to!"

Jessica felt her face grow prickly hot. She glared at him, humiliated and furious, as she gathered up her photographs. And she stalked out of the room, vowing never to speak to Cameron again.

COVER
GIRLS

**Written by
Kate William**

**Created by
FRANCINE PASCAL**

BANTAM BOOKS
NEW YORK · TORONTO · LONDON · SYDNEY · AUCKLAND

RL 6, age 12 and up

COVER GIRLS

A Bantam Book / March 1997

Sweet Valley High® is a registered trademark of Francine Pascal.
Conceived by Francine Pascal.
Produced by Daniel Weiss Associates, Inc.
33 West 17th Street
New York, NY 10011.
Cover photography by Michael Segal.

ISBN: 0-553-57063-3

Published simultaneously in the United States and Canada

Bantam Books are published by Bantam Books, a division of Bantam
Doubleday Dell Publishing Group, Inc. Its trademark, consisting of the
words "Bantam Books" and the portrayal of a rooster, is Registered in U.S.
Patent and Trademark Office and in other countries. Marca Registrada.
Bantam Books, 1540 Broadway, New York, New York 10036.

PRINTED IN THE UNITED STATES OF AMERICA

OPM   0 9 8 7 6 5 4 3 2 1

To James Ryan

Chapter 1

Elizabeth Wakefield pushed a strand of her long blond hair behind her ear as she scanned the bookshelves. "Here's the book about women in Victorian England," she said. She selected a paperback and handed it to Enid Rollins. "That's on your list, isn't it?"

Enid's green eyes sparkled. "Yes, this is one of the Morgan Agency's books," she said, thumbing through it. "And look: The author thanks one of my new bosses in the acknowledgments!"

Maria Slater grabbed the book from her and looked down at her friends with a fake haughty expression. "Special thanks to my agent, Roberta Morgan, for her expert advice and invaluable assistance," she read aloud in a pretentious English accent that made Elizabeth and Enid giggle. Maria grinned and switched back to her normal voice.

"By the time your internship at the literary agency is over," she told Enid, "authors across the country will be writing notes like this about you!"

The three Sweet Valley High juniors were standing in the women's studies section of The Book Case, a store in the mall. It was Sunday afternoon, and their school's miniterm internships were starting the next morning.

Enid laughed at Maria's confidence. "I don't think so," she said. "I doubt I'll offer much 'expert advice and invaluable assistance' in a high-school internship that lasts only two weeks!" She shook her head. Her coppery brown hair, which had only recently fully grown out after she had dyed it black some time ago, swung against her neck. "But with an accent like that, Maria, you're a shoo-in for the role of Queen Victoria!"

"I don't think the Bridgewater Theatre Group will need someone to play Queen Victoria in the next two weeks," Maria pointed out, "even if they decided to be experimental enough to cast an African American in the role."

"With your experience?" Enid argued. "They'd cast you in a minute—in any role."

"Whatever," Maria said, rolling her dark brown eyes. "Anyhow, it takes a lot longer than two weeks to put together a production. And I'm just a little ol' student intern, not a leading lady. I'll probably be painting scenery and helping the real actors get into their costumes."

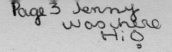

"Maybe," Elizabeth said. "But how often does a community theater get an intern with real Hollywood experience? You were the hottest child star in the country."

"I bet the actors will be asking for your autograph," Enid said confidently.

Maria frowned. "Stop! That was a long time ago," she reminded them. "And *hello!* I was the Softees toilet paper girl—I wasn't exactly performing in a play by Ibsen."

"You did movies and television too!" Elizabeth reminded her friend.

"Get over it!" Maria pleaded. "This is totally embarrassing. Besides, it's Liz's turn now! What do you think, Enid? Should we check out Elizabeth's magazine?"

"My magazine?" Elizabeth exclaimed as they walked toward the periodicals section. "It's a nice thought. But remember, I'll be a lowly editorial assistant at *Flair*, not the editor in chief!"

"Ha!" Enid said. "You're the most talented student writer in southern California. By the end of two weeks you'll be running the place!"

"That would send Todd screaming into the night," Elizabeth replied ruefully, thinking of her longtime boyfriend, Todd Wilkins. "He's already stressing about how this internship will take too much time away from him."

"He'll survive," Enid assured her.

"Todd has no right to give you attitude, Liz!"

Maria said. "He should be proud of you for hitting the big time. *Flair* is the hottest new magazine in the fashion world. It's been around less than two years. But even in New York City everyone's reading it." Maria had recently moved back to Sweet Valley after relocating with her family to New York for a few years. She and Elizabeth had been close in junior high. Now that she was back in town, she had renewed her friendship with Elizabeth. And Maria and Enid were quickly becoming friends too, although there had been some conflict between them at first.

"A magazine that popular wouldn't accept just anybody as an intern," Enid said.

Maria laughed. "They accepted Jessica, didn't they?"

"She probably impersonated Elizabeth in the interview," Enid suggested dryly. Elizabeth's identical twin sister, Jessica, had been known to borrow her sister's identity when it suited her goals.

"Jessica is such a trip," Elizabeth said, an amused grin highlighting a dimple in her left cheek. "Her internship position is photographer's assistant, but she plans to convince the photographer to make her a model and put her on the cover of the magazine. You know how much Jess loves being in the limelight."

"It's not all it's cracked up to be," Maria said seriously.

4

"Speaking of Liz's evil twin, *look*," Enid whispered urgently.

All three girls turned to see Jessica Wakefield entering the store, accompanied by her best friend, Lila Fowler.

"If it isn't Tweedledum and Tweedledummer!" Maria teased. "I never expected to see them putting in a cameo here. I'd have thought those two were allergic to bookstores."

"No, no—Jessica can do bookstores all right," Elizabeth joked, "as long as she stays in the magazine section. History gives her hives, and reference books make her sneeze."

To most customers in the store the sixteen-year-old Wakefield twins would have looked absolutely identical at first glance. Both had California tans, sun-streaked hair, and eyes the color of the Pacific Ocean. Both were five-foot six and had trim, athletic figures.

But Elizabeth, always the practical twin, had pulled her hair back in barrettes. For her trip to the mall she'd worn a denim skirt with a hemline just above her knees, a white T-shirt, and no makeup except a touch of lip gloss.

Jessica's hair was loose and as meticulously tousled as a movie star's. Her makeup was carefully applied, including a hint of violet eye shadow that was her latest cosmetic experiment. Her floral minidress left her shoulders bare, and her high-heeled sandals were the same shade as her eye shadow.

Even if they'd been dressed identically, the twins' classmates could have told them apart the instant either twin opened her mouth. Both were articulate. But Jessica's favorite topics of conversation included boys, clothes, parties, and cheerleading. Elizabeth was more likely to be heard advising a friend on a personal problem, conducting an interview for an article in the school newspaper, discussing a book with a classmate, or raising money for charity.

Despite their differences, each twin knew she could count on her sister when she was in trouble. But it was usually Jessica, the younger sister by four minutes, who got herself into ridiculous situations and needed her more sensible sister to bail her out. Elizabeth sighed as she continued walking toward the magazine racks. Sure enough, Jessica and Lila were standing in front of a brilliantly colored display of fashion and beauty magazines. Elizabeth hoped her twin wouldn't find a way to turn the internship into another one of her disasters.

"Yo, Lizzie!" Jessica called, holding up a magazine. Elizabeth winced at the hated nickname but let it slide. "Did you see the new issue of *Flair*?" Jessica asked.

"That's Simone on the cover," Maria said, sticking her nose up in the air as she emphasized the model's name. "I read that she moved to Los Angeles recently—just after Mode, the company that publishes *Flair*, moved its headquarters here. Simone was totally big in New York last year."

Enid laughed as she took the magazine from Jessica. "Big? She looks like she wears about a size one! I've never seen anyone so emaciated in my life."

"You can never be too thin or too rich," Lila reminded them haughtily. "But especially rich."

"Please!" Jessica complained, grabbing the magazine back from Enid. "We can't all have multimillionaire parents like you, Lila." She stared thoughtfully at the sophisticated, black-haired model on the cover. "But maybe you *can* be too thin. Guys can't possibly think women like Simone are sexy. Can they?" Her voice sounded worried.

"A lot of them do," said Maria. She grinned evilly. "Especially after her plastic surgery."

"What plastic surgery?" Jessica demanded. "Tell me!"

"I don't know, really," Maria said. "But there have been rumors."

"Well, I can't believe a guy would find her sexier than someone like me," Jessica insisted. "I mean, she's attractive, I guess. But she looks more like a department store mannequin than a real person!"

Elizabeth shrugged. "Don't worry about it, Jess. The boys who really count—nice boys like Todd—care more about who you are than what you look like."

7

"*Nice* isn't at the top of my wish list for a guy, Lizzie," Jessica reminded her.

"You are so *naive*, Elizabeth," Lila told her, holding out her hand wordlessly until Jessica passed her the issue of *Flair*. "Guys are letches. The point is to get what you can out of them." She gestured with the magazine. "Obviously Simone has found the look that works for her. You'd be surprised at how many men would fall all over themselves trying to get close to somebody famous and glamorous. Not my darling Bo, of course," Lila amended, speaking of her boyfriend in Washington, D.C., Beauregard Creighton the Third. "He's hopelessly devoted to me. But most guys would."

"But Liz is totally right about wimpy old Todd," Jessica said with a sigh, shaking her head at the thought of her sister's long-term relationship. "I've told you over and over again, Liz. Todd may be a hunk. But you're too young to be tied down to somebody so boring!" She turned to Lila. "Todd Wilkins doesn't have the imagination to drool over supermodels like Simone."

"*Imagination?*" Maria asked with a hoot, swiping the magazine from Lila. "This bikini Simone is wearing doesn't leave much to a guy's imagination. But Todd doesn't need to drool over supermodels. He's in love with Elizabeth—" She smiled loyally at her friend. "And Liz is as gorgeous as any supermodel."

"I really may vomit—," Lila began.

8

"I guess I'm not up on my supermodels," Enid interrupted. "I know I've seen this girl's face—or should I say her *pout*? But exactly who is she? Simone who?"

"She's just *Simone*," Lila said, as if Enid should have known. "When you're that famous, who needs a last name?"

"This will be me someday," Jessica bragged. She took the magazine from Maria and stared at it as if trying to imagine her own face on the cover. "All over the world my adoring fans will know me only as *Jessica*. Or should I use *Jesse*? Does that sound more sophisticated?"

Lila shook her head. "Jessica Wakefield, you are the most conceited person I've ever met."

"And you are the expert," Jessica interjected.

Lila stared at Jessica coldly for a moment before turning to Elizabeth, Enid, and Maria. "You should have seen Jessica this afternoon, making a photo album of herself! Have you ever heard of anything so vain?"

"You can call it vain," Jessica said. "I call it enterprising. I need a proper portfolio ready when Quentin Berg discovers me."

Enid sighed. "Again I'm clueless. What's a *Quentin Berg*?"

Jessica's mouth dropped open in shock. "Quentin Berg is only the coolest photographer in the fashion business," she told Enid. "And he's under contract to *Flair* magazine."

9

"Jessica's about to become his assistant," Elizabeth explained, taking the magazine from her. "I feel sorry for the poor man."

"Ha, ha," Jessica said flatly. "You won't be making fun of me when he promotes me from camera carrier to cover girl."

Elizabeth tuned out her sister's prattling and thumbed through the cosmetics advertisements in the front of the magazine until she came to the staff listing. "This is it!" she cried excitedly. "This is the first issue of *Flair* with the new managing editor listed. Her name is Leona Peirson. All I know about her is that she's young to be in such a high-powered position and that everyone says she's got a brilliant career in publishing ahead of her."

"Is she your new boss?" Maria asked.

Elizabeth nodded. "I can't wait to meet her. This internship is what I've been dreaming of my entire life!"

A few hours later Todd sat with Elizabeth in the front seat of his BMW, gazing over the lights of Sweet Valley. They were parked at their favorite spot on Miller's Point, and Todd was kissing her passionately, but Elizabeth seemed preoccupied. Finally she pushed him away.

"What's the matter?" Todd asked, annoyed and mystified. "Did I do something wrong? Is it my breath?"

Elizabeth smiled. "No, you're still the world's

number-one kisser. I'm just distracted tonight."

"Let me guess," Todd said with a groan as his good mood evaporated. "You're thinking about that magazine."

"Sorry," she replied, smiling wanly at him. "I've been looking forward to the miniterm for so long that I can hardly believe it starts tomorrow. Todd, I'm going to be working on a national magazine! Do you know what that means?"

Todd slouched in his seat with his arms crossed in front of him. "It means we'll have to go for two whole weeks without being able to see each other at school," he said. "What's so awesome about that?"

"Think about what a great opportunity this is!" Elizabeth urged. "For both of us," she added quickly, running her fingers playfully through his wavy brown hair.

"Right," Todd replied grumpily. "I'll be an intern at my dad's company—big deal. I already know everyone at Varitronics. And I've spent the last few months listening to my father talk about everything that goes on there. This internship will be the thrill of my life."

"You could have applied for a position somewhere more interesting," Elizabeth reminded him.

Todd rolled his eyes. "You don't seem to realize that most of the kids in our class think this miniterm thing is a joke! So does the rest of the world, for that matter."

11

"That's not true!" Elizabeth protested.

"Why do you suppose so many of us are working for our parents' firms?" he asked. "Even Lila Fowler is working at Fowler Enterprises. I'll bet Jessica isn't letting her forget that!"

Elizabeth laughed. "My sister never passes up an opportunity to gloat—especially over Lila."

"When it comes to exciting internships, you and Jess are the exceptions," Todd said. He sighed miserably, but deep down he knew that his boring internship was his own fault. He'd been too busy with basketball finals to think about applying anywhere until it was much too late. Still, it hurt to admit that he'd screwed up. And plenty of kids had applied early and still ended up with boring prospects. "How many adults with really neat careers are willing to baby-sit high-school students for two weeks?" he asked.

Elizabeth's blue-green eyes were beginning to show annoyance. "It's not baby-sitting!" she insisted. "And it's not just me and Jess who are working at something we're interested in. Aaron Dallas managed to find a great internship!"

"Don't remind me," Todd said, hating himself for being so jealous of his friend Aaron. "While I'm photocopying invoices for my father, Aaron will be working for the L.A. Lakers! And you'll be throwing yourself into that magazine the same way you always do with new activities. Plus you'll be commuting all the way to Los Angeles. I'll be lucky if you have time to see a movie with me over the weekend."

Todd knew it wasn't like him to be so negative, but he couldn't help it. He felt like an idiot for the way he'd neglected to plan ahead for the miniterm. And the thought of not seeing Elizabeth every day for the next two weeks made every muscle in his body tense up. "Life isn't fair," he concluded.

"You aren't being fair either," Elizabeth said. "Todd, I'm *excited* about this internship! Can't you please be happy for me?"

He smiled weakly. "I guess I am," he admitted. "But you may be getting your hopes up for nothing. What if you spend the whole two weeks answering the phone? It's not like anyone's going to let a sixteen-year-old make real decisions."

Elizabeth bit her lip, and Todd knew he'd struck a nerve. But she recovered quickly. "Even if I'm only answering the phone, I'll be watching and learning from real professionals," she said philosophically.

"It's not like you've never worked on a professional publication before," Todd pointed out. "You've written articles for the *Sweet Valley News* and even the *Los Angeles Times*. And you and Jessica had internships at that newspaper in London last summer. Look what happened there—you forgot all about me, you started dating some wacky poet, and you nearly got yourself killed!"

Elizabeth winced. "Well, the newspaper part was good experience anyway. And I promise the other part will not happen this time!"

"How can you be so sure?" Todd demanded.

"I learned my lesson about dating guys at the office," Elizabeth assured him with a peck on the cheek. "I'm not interested in anyone but you. And *Flair* magazine doesn't even cover serial murders! The biggest danger on this internship is the risk of having my face break out from reviewing too many makeup samples."

"But will I see you at all in the next two weeks?"

"Absolutely," Elizabeth promised. "No matter how exciting life is in the world of high fashion, I'll always have time for you."

"I certainly hope so," Todd said, grudgingly accepting another kiss.

Chapter 2

Jessica felt her sister's tug on her backpack. It was Monday morning, and the twins were walking along a sidewalk in downtown Los Angeles. Just ahead was the front entrance of the high-rise that housed *Flair* and Mode's other publications.

"For someone wearing four-inch heels, you're moving as fast as an Olympic track star," Elizabeth complained. "Wait up!"

Jessica smiled and shrugged, but she forced her feet to match Elizabeth's slower pace. "I can't help it!" she said, admiring her new Italian platform shoes. She couldn't afford them, of course. But it would be weeks before her mother received the credit card bill. By then, Jessica was sure she'd be on her way to a lucrative career as a supermodel.

"I'm anxious to get there too," Elizabeth said, her voice quavering slightly. Jessica felt some

15

nervous energy about their first day on the job, but Elizabeth, she realized, was downright tense.

"I am so excited about *Flair* magazine, Liz. This is the most awesome job we've ever had!" Jessica exclaimed. "Anyhow, you're just jealous of my shoes. I mean, well . . ." Her mouth twisted with distaste as she pointed to Elizabeth's simple, low-heeled navy pumps.

"What's wrong with my shoes?" Elizabeth asked, her voice several tones higher than usual.

"Well, nothing's *wrong* with them, exactly," Jessica said, trying to be reassuring. "But they're so . . . middle management."

"What's that supposed to mean?" Elizabeth asked, mystified. "They're practical, and they're a classic design. Two years from now I'll still be wearing these shoes. In six months those stacked heels of yours will be out of style."

"So what's your point?" Jessica asked. "When platform shoes are out of style, I'll just buy something different. That's how fashion works!"

"Never mind," Elizabeth said miserably, gesturing for Jessica to precede her through the revolving door.

Jessica nudged Elizabeth as they stepped onto the shiny marble floor inside. "Look at the way they're all dressed!" she whispered, nodding across the huge lobby toward a group of sleek, well-groomed women waiting for the elevator, as well as a few men. Almost all the women wore long, body-hugging jackets with miniskirts.

"They don't look very businesslike," Elizabeth noted, whispering back to her sister as the twins stopped near the entrance to watch the stylish group. "Those short little skirts are so tight, they could have been painted on! How do they sit down? And why are they all wearing purple lipstick?"

"You are so *last season*, Liz," Jessica remarked. "That's not purple. Nobody wears purple lipstick anymore. That's *plum!* It's all the rage. And look at the metallic gold eye shadow. That is *so cool!*"

"I thought you were wearing nothing but violet eye shadow from now on," Elizabeth reminded her.

Jessica rolled her eyes. *"Please,"* she said, dismissing the fashion trend she'd been raving about for a week. "Honestly, Liz—do you really think I'd wear eye shadow that clashed with the new plum lipstick I'm going to buy?"

"Horrors!" Elizabeth said. "I can't keep up with crazy trends. They change too fast for me. Anyhow, I bet all those women are models. Nobody else could get away with clothes and makeup like that in the office."

"Look at the way most of them are wearing their hair—longer in the front," Jessica observed, pulling wings of hair straight on both sides of her face. "Tomorrow I'm going to find a way to make mine look that way. Maybe if I curl it some in back

17

and use a ton of mousse to get these pieces perfectly straight—"

"You're only working here for two weeks, Jessica," Elizabeth pointed out. "Does it really matter if your hair is just like everyone else's?"

"It won't be just like everyone else's," Jessica said impatiently. "Mine is naturally blond. And it's important to be in style when you're working in the fashion industry. C'mon, Liz. Your skirt is tons longer than those skirts. And do you think I'm OK in a pantsuit instead of a skirt?"

"My navy suit is classic. It should be fine for any office situation," Elizabeth said staunchly. "I wasn't sure about those pants of yours, to tell you the truth. They're awfully tight for the office—or so I thought. But if those women can get away with skirts the size of headbands, nobody can say *you're* inappropriate."

Jessica appraised her own outfit critically. "I'll wear a miniskirt tomorrow instead of pants," she decided. "But my jacket's tailored like their jackets. And my black pants are almost as close-fitting as those black tights those women are all wearing. I think my clothes will do. At least they make a statement."

"And what statement am I making?" Elizabeth asked, glancing down at her conservative suit with a new uncertainty in her blue-green eyes.

Jessica thought her sister's boringly correct suit made only one statement: *I am hopelessly dowdy.*

And Elizabeth's hair, pinned up with barrettes, looked high-schoolish. But Jessica smiled reassuringly. "Chill out, Liz," she said. "You're right. Those women probably *are* models. If I want Quentin Berg to make me a cover girl, I have to dress like them. But you're working in an office where a bunch of brainiac writer types will be sitting in front of computers. I doubt they'll be as trendy as those of us in the art department."

The first group had vanished into the sleek, shining elevator. But another group was gathering as Elizabeth and Jessica stepped toward the mirrored doors. Again almost every woman wore a miniskirt and a fitted blazer.

As the girls walked with them into the elevator Jessica noticed one woman gazing coldly at her. She was in her forties and ultraslim, with long tendrils of chestnut hair curled under so that they nearly touched her chin. The woman looked Jessica up and down. "Aggressive choice," she pronounced finally, her voice low and throaty.

Jessica wasn't sure if it was a compliment, but she decided to take it as one. She nodded slightly, allowing the faintest of disdainful smiles to tug at the corners of her mouth. Fashion models didn't grin.

Elizabeth gulped as the women in the elevator gazed coldly from the top of Jessica's tousled blond head to the rounded tips of her black-and-cranberry platform shoes. After a moment they looked away again, as if their curiosity was satis-fied. Every set of gold-shadowed eyes pivoted back to the display of numbers above the elevator door. Nobody else said a word. And nobody even glanced at Elizabeth. She wasn't sure if that was a good sign or a bad one. When she'd left the house this morning, she'd felt stylish and professional in her blue suit. Now she felt invisible.

Elizabeth seldom sought out the limelight. But total invisibility was a new sensation, and it made her uneasy. Being an identical twin—and an attrac-tive, blond identical twin—usually caught people's eye. She told herself that it didn't matter. Her writ-ing and proofreading skills would be more impor-tant to Leona Peirson than the length of her blazer. But her elation about the internship had abruptly shifted to terror.

Elizabeth envied her sister's composure. Quietly humming to herself, Jessica looked as though she was born to ride in an elevator with these svelte, plum-lipped denizens of the fashion world. Elizabeth shifted her weight from one sen-sibly clad foot to the other, squeezing the leather handle of her briefcase with both hands as she stared at the greenish numbers above the elevator doors.

The crowded elevator stopped at the ninth floor, where *Flair*'s art department was located. Jessica squeezed her sister's shoulder. "Relax, Liz. You'll do fine," she whispered into

Elizabeth's ear. Then Jessica added in a louder voice, "See you at lunchtime!" as she bounced out of the elevator.

All the men and a few of the women Elizabeth had pegged as models also stepped out. But most of the fashionable women stayed, and Elizabeth had the depressing feeling that they were all headed for the editorial offices, on the eleventh floor. As the doors glided shut, separating her from Jessica's stylish pants and tousled hair, Elizabeth suddenly felt very much alone.

A few minutes later, on the eleventh floor, an administrative assistant pointed out Leona Peirson's office and told Elizabeth to walk right in. A tall woman stood with her back to the door, her dark blond hair slightly longer in the front. She wore a black pinstripe miniskirt with a matching tailored blazer the same length as the skirt.

"I'm Elizabeth Wakefield," Elizabeth said, glad that her voice was steadier than her trembling knees. "I'm the new student intern."

The woman turned around, and Elizabeth was horrified to see that she'd interrupted a phone call. But Leona Peirson smiled broadly, as if genuinely glad to see her new intern. Elizabeth began to back out of the office until the tall woman gestured toward a chair. Elizabeth sat down gratefully. For the first time since she'd entered the lobby of the building, she began to relax.

*　　*　　*

Jessica glided into the hallway leading to Quentin Berg's studio. Her backpack dangled from one hand, and she walked with her hips thrust forward like a model on a runway. A photographer had once told her she was too short, at five-foot six, to be a fashion model. But she was sure that a maverick like Quentin Berg could see beyond that tiny little deficiency and appreciate her unique spark. "And if he can't, well, that's what the four-inch heels are for," she whispered under her breath.

The studio was a cavernous room with a jumble of ladders, props, and lights near the far end and a couch in one corner. Open doors showed glimpses of offices, meeting spaces, smaller studios, and storage areas beyond the main room. Jessica could hear people bustling around in those rooms and at the far end of the main studio. But it wouldn't do for her to seek anyone out. Like the elevator women, she would be stylishly aloof.

She sauntered to the center of the room and pivoted there, as if inspecting her surroundings, with a vague look of boredom. Four youngish-looking men were climbing the ladders, assembling the props, and adjusting some bluish lights a few yards away. Jessica was careful not to look directly at them. But she made sure they had a good view of her.

She gave them a moment to admire her body-hugging outfit, her movie-star hair, and her flawless face. Nobody even glanced up. A moment later the four men finished their work and hurried out of the room.

Through several of the open doors Jessica watched the four men and various other people hurrying in and out of adjoining rooms. Most seemed intent on moving props and lights around. Jessica was beginning to get annoyed. Either she was losing her famous Wakefield charisma or these guys were too stupid to realize that admiring a sexy blonde was more interesting than draping muslin over a ladder.

Suddenly Jessica knew how Elizabeth had felt when the women in the elevator had ignored her. Well, nobody ignored Jessica Wakefield for long. *Ever.*

She cleared her throat loudly, and a guy's head popped into the room through one of the open doorways. He was almost young—no more than twenty-five. And he was wearing overalls with a safari-looking vest. His outfit was kind of grunge, Jessica decided. She figured he had to be some sort of assistant photographer. But he was good-looking, in a stylish kind of way, with thick reddish blond hair and nice broad shoulders. So she struck a casual pose and waited breathlessly while his eyes traveled up and down her body.

"Are you the intern?" he asked in a deep voice, standing in the doorway.

Jessica decided aloofness worked only on women. She flashed him her most dazzling smile. "Yes," she said. "I'm Jessica Wake—"

"Get me coffee!" he barked, cutting her off. He spun on the heel of his work boot and disappeared through the door.

Jessica followed him. "Who are you to be giving me orders?" she demanded.

"I'm Quentin Berg, your *boss*," he said. He pointed toward a coffee machine in the corner of the room. *"Now move!"*

Jessica gasped in fury. Then she whirled around and stomped off toward the coffee machine, her platform soles thumping loudly on the wood floor. Her internship wasn't starting off exactly the way she'd imagined.

So far, Todd's internship was even duller than he'd expected. He sat in his windowless cubicle at Varitronics, checking the sales numbers on a draft memo against a sea of tiny figures on a green-and-white-striped spreadsheet printout. In two hours on the job the most exciting task he'd handled was making lunch reservations for his father and one of the vice presidents. And when his father was too busy to assign him tasks, he was at the beck and call of Margaret Meeks, the tyrannical administrative assistant for the executive suite.

It was only ten o'clock on Monday morning.

But it already seemed as if the day had dragged on forever.

Todd rubbed his deep brown eyes. The tiny print was making him see double. He turned to his blank computer screen. THIS JOB REEKS! he typed in capital letters. Certainly it was time for his ten-minute coffee break.

With a guilty glance around him Todd deleted the line from his computer screen. Then he unfolded his cramped legs and rose slowly to his full height of six-foot three. The creaky chair had surely been designed for miniature office workers. Todd would never have guessed that his father could subject him to such torture, on top of the stupid spreadsheets. Bert Wilkins was usually such a kind, reasonable man.

Either Dad secretly morphs into Sadistic Psycho Boss whenever he walks into this building, Todd thought, *or he's gone overboard trying to show his staff that the president's son doesn't get special treatment.* Either way, Todd didn't think he could stand another nine days, five hours, and fifty-six minutes of slaving away at his father's firm.

To make matters worse, the Varitronics dress code required everyone to wear a suit—even the high-school intern. Margaret's hawklike eyes followed Todd as he walked across the room to the coffee counter. He wanted to yell, "What are you looking at? Haven't you ever seen somebody take a coffee break before?"

Instead he tugged impatiently at his too-tight tie, wondering if anyone had ever died from being strangled by paisleys. Thinking of his tie made Todd think of Elizabeth, who'd surprised him with the fashionable instrument of torture for his sixteenth birthday. In all honesty, he reminded himself, he'd always loved the paisley tie. But today nothing felt right. He realized that he missed Elizabeth terribly, even though he'd seen her only twelve hours earlier. He hoped she was having a more exciting morning at *Flair* than he was at Varitronics.

He stood near one of the room's few windows, gulping the bitter black coffee and wishing it were root beer. He felt the administrative assistant's glare on his back, but he decided to ignore it. If Meeks had more work for him to do, she would have to wait until his coffee break was over.

As he turned toward the coffeemaker to contemplate a second cup his eyes fell on the fax machine in the corner of the room. For the first time all morning Todd smiled a genuine smile. The internship meant he couldn't see Elizabeth during the day. And someone might overhear him if he called his girlfriend on the phone during company time. But that didn't mean he couldn't let her know he was thinking about her.

Elizabeth's eyes widened when Leona Peirson hung up the telephone and turned toward her. The managing editor of *Flair* magazine was even younger than Elizabeth had imagined—twenty-nine or thirty, Elizabeth guessed, looking at the woman's slender figure and unlined face.

The editor smiled again and grasped Elizabeth's hand in a firm handshake. "I'm Leona Peirson," she said unnecessarily. "I'm fairly new in this position myself, so don't feel intimidated about dropping by to ask questions. Sometimes we might just have to discover the answers together."

"Ms. Peirson," Elizabeth began. "I want you to know how grateful I am—"

"Please call me Leona," the editor interrupted, her brown eyes warm. "And no thanks are necessary. I consider us a team, Elizabeth. I know from your application that you're here because you truly want the experience of working on a professional magazine. I'll consider my time with you well spent if you work hard and learn a lot in the next few weeks. I expect you might even teach us a thing or two."

"I doubt that," Elizabeth said modestly. "I've never had any experience with magazines, only newspapers. But I promise you that I'll work hard at whatever you ask me to do."

Leona leaned back in her chair and looked thoughtfully at her new intern. "I have every confidence that you will," she said. "I can't promise that all the work will be glamorous. A lot of the tasks that go into putting a magazine together are what we call 'scum' work. You'll spend some of your time opening mail, proofreading articles, and fact checking product information."

"Oh, I don't mind at all," Elizabeth said, mesmerized by the aura of confidence Leona projected. "I want to get experience in all areas of publishing."

"I'm glad to hear that," Leona said. "Because it's the only way to get a realistic picture of what it's like to be a magazine professional. At the same time I think we might find some real writing or substantive editing for you to do now and then as well."

Elizabeth beamed.

"I want your input, Elizabeth," Leona continued, ticking off points on her fingers. "I welcome your ideas, so don't be shy about speaking out. I like to see creativity and hard work rewarded. My other ground rule is to tell me what's really on your mind—no hiding the truth if you have a problem. As long as we're both completely honest with each other we should get along wonderfully. Am I making myself clear?"

"Absolutely," Elizabeth said, feeling as if this internship really could be the start of a lifelong career. The insecurity she'd felt on the elevator was gone, banished by Leona's powerful presence. The editor was obviously an assertive, intelligent woman who knew how to get where she wanted to go. And she seemed truly interested in helping Elizabeth forge a career.

"Your office is just around the corner from mine," Leona said as she walked out from behind her desk and guided Elizabeth toward the door.

"My *office?*" Elizabeth asked, her eyes wide. "I assumed I'd sit in a cubicle somewhere."

Leona smiled. "One of our associate editors is out on family leave for several months, so we've given you his office," she said. "I want you to spend the next hour or two familiarizing yourself with the magazine. A stack of back issues is on the desk for you to look through."

"I'll get right to it," Elizabeth said with a nod.

"Oh, and Elizabeth . . . ," Leona began as Elizabeth left the room. "I don't mean to be critical. But you might want to pay a little more attention to your wardrobe," she suggested. "I'm sure the navy suit would be fine in most workplaces. But this is a *fashion* magazine."

Elizabeth nodded again, blushing. As she hurried out of Leona's office she wished, for once, that she had Jessica's sense of style—though not even Jessica was dressed in as sophisticated a manner as the goddesses of style who roamed the halls of *Flair.* But Elizabeth vowed that she would find a way to impress her new boss. Working for Leona Peirson was a dream come true. Elizabeth would do whatever she could to be worthy of her attention.

Chapter 3

"Hold the elevator!" Jessica called to Shelly Fabian, a makeup artist who prepared many of Quentin Berg's models. Shelly lunged for the keypad, and two long, skinny braids swung around her face with a bright tinkle of glass beads.

Jessica hobbled onto the elevator just as the doors slid shut. "Thanks, Shelly," she said with a groan. She let her backpack slide to the floor. Then she slipped off one Italian platform shoe and massaged her cramped toes, ignoring the cold glare of a sleek, burgundy-haired woman who stood in the corner of the elevator, dressed entirely in black. Jessica couldn't wait to get to the cafeteria and pour out her troubles into Elizabeth's sympathetic ear.

"Already among the walking wounded, Jessica?" Shelly asked, checking her ebony-skinned reflection in the mirrored elevator door. "It's only noon!"

Jessica caught sight of her own straggly hair in the door and quickly turned away. It was better not to think about how messy and sweaty she looked. "After this morning my feet are screaming four-letter words at me!" Jessica replied. "I broke two nails moving a three-ton lighting array back and forth across the room."

"Quentin's not the most decisive person in the world when it comes to where to put his props," Shelly said.

"I could tell him where to put a few," Jessica said mock threateningly. "Is it always so crazy in the art department?"

Shelly laughed knowingly. "It's going to get a lot crazier after lunch, when we actually do the big shoot!" she warned. Her voice dropped to a whisper, and she spoke close to Jessica's ear. "Just wait until the toothpick chicks show up! Get a few of those skinny prima donna models in the studio, and you'll be taking orders from a bevy of spoiled brats as well as Quentin."

"That settles it," Jessica replied. "I've got to find a way to become a leggy supermodel in the next hour. I wasn't cut out for manual labor."

"At least you can say things like that without being laughed at," said Shelly, smoothing her hands ruefully over her own ample hips under her requisite miniskirt. The makeup artist was about thirty-five, and Jessica had to admit that she was overweight, but her legs were as great as any model's. "As for the manual labor," Shelly continued, "all you can do is grin and bear it."

"I tried that once before," Jessica said with a grimace. "For about a week, when I was suffering from temporary insanity, I was a roadie for this totally gross rock band called Spontaneous Combustion. I didn't think life could get any worse than lugging amplifiers around. Today it did. At least I wasn't wearing four-inch heels for Spy and Wheels."

"You worked with people named Spy and Wheels?" Shelly asked. "I hope they were hunks at least."

Jessica shuddered. "I'd rather kiss a cockroach!" she said. "These guys made my skin crawl."

"That's one thing Quentin has over them," Shelly said. "He's definitely a hunk—until he opens his mouth," she added in a whisper.

The elevator stopped at the second floor. "Can you point me toward the company cafeteria?" Jessica asked.

"I can do better than that," Shelly said with a smile. "I can walk you there. I'm meeting a friend for lunch."

"I'm meeting my sister," Jessica said, hoisting her backpack again and wondering if someone had slipped a few bricks into it. As they entered the busy lunchroom she caught sight of a wall clock. "Liz is probably here somewhere, freaking out because I'm ten minutes late," she told Shelly with a sigh. "My sister has a terminal case of punctuality."

Shelly caught sight of her date and waved across the room. "Have a good lunch!" she told Jessica. She wiggled her eyebrows comically. "But whatever you do, don't eat the chicken potpie!"

Jessica collapsed into the nearest chair, surprised to realize that Elizabeth hadn't arrived yet. *When Liz shows up, I'll make her go through the cafeteria line for me,* she decided silently. *I'm too tired to move.*

A moment later Elizabeth rushed into the cafeteria. Jessica brightened up when she saw her sister. A little pampering was exactly what she needed, and Elizabeth was one of the most sensitive, helpful people she knew.

"Sorry I'm late, Jess!" Elizabeth exclaimed, her voice frantic but happy. "I am having the most exciting—"

"Man, am I glad you're here!" Jessica began. "You are so lucky to be sitting at a desk all day. My feet are going to sue me for assault. So while you're getting your own lunch, would you—"

"I can't stay!" Elizabeth said. "I'm going to grab a salad and eat at my desk. I'll talk to you tonight!" She whirled away, blond hair flying, before Jessica could say another word.

Elizabeth waited breathlessly for the letter she'd just drafted to come out of the printer. She skimmed it quickly and raced around the corner to her boss's office. Leona wasn't there, so Elizabeth dropped the letter in the in-box on her desk.

The letter informed a writer that her manuscript was unacceptable, but that Leona would reconsider it if she'd make certain changes. It wasn't a complicated letter, but it was Elizabeth's first tangible product as a member of a professional magazine staff, and she'd worked hard to get the tone just right. Now she just had to wait for Leona's opinion of her work. By her usual standards the letter was a good one. But was it good enough for *Flair*? She had no way of knowing except to wait for Leona's verdict. And that might be hours away. Elizabeth took a deep breath and forced herself to walk slowly back to her own office.

A few minutes later Elizabeth was sitting at her desk. As she finished up the salad she'd bought for lunch, she studied a back issue of *Flair* that she'd draped over the keyboard of her computer. She looked up to see a young Asian woman standing in the doorway.

"Hi! You must be Elizabeth, the new intern," the woman said, a smile lighting her features. She held out something wrapped in a napkin. "I'm Reggie Andrews. Would you like a cookie? They're chocolate chip."

Elizabeth grinned. "I'd love one. They're my favorite."

Reggie was several inches shorter than Elizabeth, with almond-shaped eyes and a flawless complexion. Her straight black hair was a little shorter than Elizabeth's. Like most of the other women at *Flair*, she wore it with long tendrils in the front. Her fine-knit sweater was of fuchsia silk, and her black leather miniskirt wasn't quite as short as most of the other skirts Elizabeth had seen at the office. Elizabeth was sure that a long, fitted blazer was draped over a chair in Reggie's office.

"I'm an assistant fashion editor here," Reggie said. "But I started out last year, after I graduated college, as an editorial assistant. So I have a pretty good idea what you're in for in the next few weeks. If you have any questions . . ."

Elizabeth flashed her another smile. "Thanks!" she said eagerly. "I'm sure I'll have a ton of questions. I feel like a little kid, running to Leona every time I need to know something. I've been trying to ask other people too. But I'm just not comfortable yet with most of the editors."

"Would you like to have lunch together tomorrow?" Reggie asked. "We can go somewhere besides the company cafeteria. I'll fill you in on all those Things the Managers Never Tell You."

"That sounds great," Elizabeth replied. "I'm psyched to get the lowdown on what really goes on in the world of high-fashion publishing."

"It's a date!" Reggie said. "I'll stop by here

about noon, if that's OK." She turned to leave. "What's that taped to the wall over your computer?" she asked suddenly. Reggie leaned over to inspect the fax Elizabeth had received from Todd that morning. It showed a crudely drawn cartoon of a guy and a girl, each in a different workplace setting. Above the boy's head a dialogue bubble read "Your office or mine?"

"The stick person with the bow in her hair is me," Elizabeth explained. "The one with the tie is my boyfriend, Todd." She pointed to a small framed photograph of Todd that she'd placed on the corner of her desk. "Believe me, he's a better boyfriend than he is an artist!"

"Ooh!" Reggie exclaimed. "He's a *major* hunk. Much better looking than the stick-person version."

Elizabeth laughed. "Yes, he is, isn't he?"

Reggie turned back to the fax and read aloud the note he'd scrawled beneath the cartoon: "Elizabeth, I'm sorry I've been a jerk. I guess I can share you with the fashion world for two weeks. You've got too much talent to waste. I hope your internship is everything you want it to be. Love, Todd." Reggie seemed genuinely touched. "Oh, Elizabeth. That's so sweet! That's a pretty special guy you've got. It sounds like you two have a wonderful relationship."

Elizabeth experienced the same warm glow she'd felt when she'd first seen the fax. "He is special," she agreed. "In fact, I'm meeting him for a soda tonight at nine. It's the only time we could work out. We won't see all that much of each other during our two-week internships. But nothing can really come between us."

"It's almost one-fifteen," Shelly said to Jessica that afternoon in the photography studio. For the moment the two women were alone in the main studio. "The models for the big photo shoot will be here in a half hour. If I were you, I'd be sure the set is ready. Quentin will pitch a fit if a single one of those fake rocks is out of place."

Jessica rolled her eyes. "Fake?" she asked, struggling to get her arms around a faux boulder the size of an ottoman. "Believe me, these things are just as heavy as the real thing. *Argh!*" she exclaimed suddenly, her voice rising. She dropped the fake rock.

"Are you all right?" Shelly asked, concerned.

"No!" Jessica wailed. "I broke another nail!"

"You'll break more before the day is through," Shelly predicted as she turned back to the makeup trays she was setting out in one corner of the room for touch-ups on the set.

"Why is Quentin using rocks in a fashion spread?" Jessica asked. "Who's modeling the new fall line? The Flintstones?"

"Close," Shelly replied. "An up-and-coming designer, Lina Lapin, has a whole line of stuff trimmed with leather and faux fur. I guess Quentin thinks the rocks will give it that natural look. He plans to pose Simone and another female model there, surrounded by admiring guys—all of them dressed in Lapin designs with fake leopard and tiger skins."

"It sounds majorly stupid," Jessica said, painfully hoisting the rock back up and eyeing the distance it had to be moved.

Shelly shrugged. "I'd say the same thing except I've seen him pull off weirder ideas than this. Quentin may be an arrogant louse—you didn't hear that from me, by the way—but he does have good instincts for what will look great in a fashion spread. Besides, he didn't design the clothes."

Jessica dropped the fake rock with a thud. She tried to nudge it into place with her foot but only succeeded in bursting one of her new blisters. She stifled a cry and sat down hard on the rock. "I bet he designed these stupid *rocks*—just to test me! I've *got* to find a way to become a model instead of bulldozer. This body was not made for heavy lifting."

Shelly laughed. "Your *shoes* certainly weren't," she said. "Jessica, I hate to disillusion you. But photography assistants don't get promoted to model. That's not the career path. It just doesn't happen."

"Well, I intend to *make* it happen," Jessica

vowed. "Doesn't the photographer get to choose the models? I mean, if he suddenly noticed a girl—"

Shelly shook her head. "It's a lot more complicated than that. The editors and the art director and the photographer all work with an agency to choose the models they want. The fashion designer gets involved too, if they're doing a spread on one designer's work. It's a group decision."

"But Quentin Berg is such hot stuff right now," Jessica said. "If he wanted to use one person in particular, they'd go with his choice, wouldn't they?"

"Well . . . yes," Shelly admitted. "To an extent. I mean, that's why we're using Simone so much these days. You know, she and Quentin have a thing going," she confided, raising her eyebrows suggestively. "Michael says they've been out to all the coolest nightspots in town."

"Michael who?" Jessica asked.

"Michael Rietz, the hair stylist," Shelly said. "I think you met him this morning." Jessica remembered an intense-looking guy with long dark hair who seemed to take his job very seriously. "He does the models' hair for photo shoots," Shelly explained. "Michael said Simone and Quentin were spotted together this weekend at that trendy new club, the Edge. I bet the tabloids this week will be full of pics of the Dastardly Duo, gazing adoringly at each other."

Jessica's mouth dropped open. "So *that's* the way to do it," she said, her eyes lighting up. *All I have to do is get Quentin Berg to fall in love with me.* With a top photographer at her side, gazing adoringly at her, she'd be a rich, famous super-model in no time—even at five-foot six. She could put up with dating a jerk if he was as useful—and handsome—as Quentin. "Of course," she mur-mured, half to herself. "It makes perfect sense."

"You said it," Shelly replied, misunderstanding her intent. "It makes sense for both of them. Simone gets the cover spot of *Flair* handed to her on a silver platter. And Quentin gets to be seen in public with the Fashion Witch."

"You don't think much of Simone?" Jessica asked. To carry out the plan that was forming in her mind, she would need to learn everything she could about the skinny, black-haired supermodel. "What's she like?"

Shelly glanced around to make sure they were still alone. "Simone has attitude, *big time,*" Shelly said. "She's a total brat to other women, but she acts like she's heaven's gift to men. I don't think I've ever seen her smile. She goes around with this obnoxious scowl, like she's been sucking on a lime all day."

"Sounds charming," Jessica said sarcastically.

"I don't know if it's true, but I've heard she had silicone injections to make her lips fuller," Shelly whispered. "And maybe a nose job too."

"Yuck!" Jessica exclaimed. "That lip thing hurts even just to think about. What does Quentin see in this . . . goddess?"

"A ticket to the ritziest parties in L.A.," Shelly said. "And a way to show the paparazzi types that he's made it as a photographer. I doubt he even likes her that much. She's just convenient. Anyhow, he's obnoxious too. Quentin and Simone deserve each other."

"I don't know about that—," Jessica began.

"Shhh!" hissed Shelly. "Simone's here."

A girl of about nineteen sauntered into the studio, hips first. Jessica immediately recognized her signature pout and asymmetrical haircut from the magazine covers. Simone looked even skinnier in person than she did in her photographs.

"She's got to be six feet tall," Jessica whispered, rising to her aching feet. "I've never seen a toothpick with legs before."

Simone had skin so pale that Jessica doubted it had ever seen the sun. Her lips did seem impossibly full, and they were drawn into a sensuous pout. Her sleek, unevenly cut hair was unnaturally black. She gazed at Jessica with pale blue eyes that were cold and strangely blank. Jessica loathed her at first sight.

"You," Simone said, pointing as if Jessica were a piece of furniture. "You're the intern, right?" She went on without waiting for a reply. "Go downstairs and find me some mineral water. *Now.*"

"If I were you, I'd demand a refund from that charm school," Jessica suggested under her breath. Shelly turned her face away from Simone, a hand clapped over her mouth to hide her laughter. But Jessica couldn't afford to make an enemy of Simone so soon.

"What did you say?" Simone asked, raising her skinny, highly arched eyebrows even higher. Apparently she was accustomed to having her orders carried out with no discussion.

Jessica's voice flowed like honey through her clenched jaw. "Would you prefer the mineral water that's bottled in the Rocky Mountains or the Swiss Alps?" she asked.

Simone sighed loudly. "France, of course," she announced in a pained voice. "Is there anywhere else?"

"Of course," Jessica said. *"Pardonnez-moi."* She bent again to give the fake rock one last shove into place.

"I said *now*," Simone repeated. *"Run."*

Jessica took a deep breath, and her face froze into a smile that was as genuine as the color of Simone's hair. "Yes, of course," she replied stonily.

As she stalked down the hall toward the elevator Jessica slammed her right fist into her left palm. *Stealing Quentin away from Simone will be a good start,* she decided. *But that's not enough. Somehow or other I'll bring Simone down.* Hard.

* * *

A few hours later Elizabeth hesitated in the doorway of Leona's office. "You wanted to see me?" she asked.

Leona smiled. "Come on in, Elizabeth. Please, take a seat. I wanted to talk to you about that letter you drafted for me."

"I'd be happy to make whatever changes you suggest—," Elizabeth began.

"It's excellent exactly the way it is," Leona said. "You clearly conveyed to the author my suggestions for rewriting her manuscript. And you did it tactfully and succinctly. Besides that, your spelling and grammar were flawless. You'd be surprised at how many people we get in here—even professional editors—who are careless when it comes to routine correspondence."

"Thank you," Elizabeth said, thoroughly relieved. "I always proofread everything four times."

"As a matter of fact, I'm pleased with every aspect of your first day on the job," Leona told her. "I know I've been tied up in meetings for much of the day, but you've worked well on your own, without a lot of hand-holding. You did an excellent job of proofreading the fashion-show calendar. And the other editors tell me you've taken the initiative and asked intelligent, insightful questions about what you've seen in back issues of *Flair.* I'm very impressed."

Elizabeth beamed. "I'm relieved to hear you say that," she admitted. "I was afraid I might be bothering people."

"Not at all," Leona assured her. "A successful woman isn't afraid to go out and get the information she needs to do her job and get ahead." Leona paused, staring thoughtfully at Elizabeth.

"What is it?" Elizabeth asked.

"Speaking of getting ahead," Leona began, "I just wanted to let you know that if you keep up the good work, there is a strong possibility that this magazine could offer you a real summer job when school lets out in a few months."

Elizabeth almost gasped. She had never even allowed herself to dream of a real, paid job with *Flair*. She imagined how impressive such a credential would look on a college application and what a head start it might give her after college. "Do you really think so?" she asked.

"The potential is definitely there," Leona said. "Of course, such an opportunity would require a one hundred percent commitment from you in the next two weeks. That might mean a lot of extra hours."

"Oh, I'll give you and *Flair* one hundred fifty percent!" Elizabeth assured her. "I promise you'll see just how dedicated I can be to something I care about. I'll sacrifice everything else."

As Elizabeth walked back into her own office a minute later her eyes caught sight of Todd's fax hanging over her desk. Todd's note said he was willing to share her with the magazine for two weeks. But he'd been assuming she would be free at night and on the weekend. How understanding would he be about her one hundred fifty percent commitment?

"I'll sacrifice everything else," she had promised Leona. She stared at her framed photograph of Todd and wondered exactly what that sacrifice might include.

Jessica trudged toward the mail room behind the first-floor lobby of the Mode building. The day was drawing to a close, and she'd become so used to the pain in her feet that she barely noticed it anymore. *Or maybe,* she speculated, *the pain in the rest of my body has gotten so bad that it's drowning out the screams from my new blisters.* She vowed that she would never wear the four-inch heels again.

Back in Five Minutes, read a sign on the mail-room door. Jessica pushed open the door and stared around her in surprise. Unlike the building's snazzy, sumptuous lobby and the modern, efficient art department, the mail area was a cluttered warren of storage nooks, sorting rooms, and loading docks. The place was kind of grungy, and the furnishings were decidedly run-down. But when she saw a shabby, soft-looking couch sitting empty, Jessica felt as if she'd come home. She fell onto the couch, kicked the expensive Italian torture chambers off her feet, and lay across the cushions to wait for the mail-room staff to return so she could pick up the package of prints Quentin had asked her to retrieve.

After an afternoon of running errands for both Quentin and Simone, lugging around camera equipment and fake boulders, and watching Simone preen for the lens, Jessica wished she'd never heard of *Flair* magazine. For the moment the tattered sofa felt as comfortable as her own bed—no, as comfortable as Lila's bed, with its satin sheets and mountains of pillows. *I'll just rest my eyes for a minute while I wait,* she decided, allowing her eyelids to gently fall shut.

Suddenly something brushed against her lips. Startled, Jessica popped open her eyes, and she realized she'd been asleep. A very cute guy was standing in front of her, grinning. He was tall and well built, with curly brown hair and big brown eyes that crinkled at the corners when he smiled. She guessed he was about twenty years old.

But he just kissed *me!* she thought as her brain came fully awake. Jessica sat up straight. She gulped, not sure whether to feel flattered or horrified.

"Sorry," he said with a sheepish grin. "I couldn't help it. You looked just like Sleeping Beauty, lying there with your golden hair spread out across the cushions. . . ."

"Well, I feel more like Cinderella," Jessica replied truthfully. "*Before* the fairy godmother."

He laughed. "Speaking of fairy-tale heroines,

what did Snow White say when the mail-room guy announced that her photographs hadn't arrived yet?"

Jessica raised her eyebrows. "I don't know. What?"

The guy sang in a warbling voice, "Someday my prints will come!"

"I get it." Jessica groaned. "*P-r-i-n-t-s* instead of *p-r-i-n-c-e!* That's bad. I mean, that's *really* bad!" But she couldn't help laughing.

"Good, I'm glad to see you can laugh," the guy said. "Now tell me what's wrong. What's got you feeling like you need a fairy godmother?"

"Quentin Berg," she answered testily. "Or Simone I'm-Too-Important-to-Need-a-Last-Name, queen of La-La Land. Take your pick."

"No, thank you," he said. "I don't pick either one of them. What have they done now?"

"I'm Quentin's new intern—that translates as *slave*, by the way," Jessica added. "I've always thought of myself as a slave to fashion, but this isn't what I had in mind."

"So Quentin's got you doing his heavy work?" the guy asked.

"I thought it was bad enough when it was just him ordering me around. Then Simone showed up and started playing control freak—as if I had nothing better to do than to fetch and carry for that stuck-up witch! Nobody told me that being a photography assistant included waiting on spoiled-brat models."

"If you ask me, you're worth ten of Simone," he said, leafing through a stack of bulging overnight envelopes. "She ought to be waiting on you—not the other way around."

Jessica gave the cute guy one of her most brilliant smiles. "You're obviously an extremely good judge of character," she told him.

He pulled an envelope from the stack and handed it to her. Jessica looked down in surprise. It was an overnight package addressed to Quentin. It was from the lab, and it was marked Photographs. "How did you know that this is what I came down here for?" she asked. "Are you a mind reader?"

"Absolutely," he said. "But it was Quentin's mind I read. It was very easy to do. Especially after he called down here a few minutes ago to find out—and I quote—'where in blazes that ditzy intern ran off to.' You've got to admit: The man has a way with words."

"He's channeling William Shakespeare," Jessica agreed.

"Well, he did sound a trifle vexed," the mailroom guy said in a bad British accent. "So if I were you, I'd get back up there lickety-split. Quentin can be a bear when he's irritated."

"I haven't seen him yet when he's *not* irritated!" Jessica complained. She tucked the envelope under her arm. "But you want to know the most irritating thing of all?" she called back to him as she

49

hobbled toward the door as fast as her platform shoes allowed.

"What's that?" he asked, his voice amused.

"The prints in this envelope are all of *Simone!*" Jessica said, wrinkling her nose. "This innocent-looking envelope contains dozens of copies of that smug, pouting, surgery-enhanced face!"

"Don't look at those photographs," he warned. "You'll turn to stone!"

Jessica was laughing as she waited for the elevator. It was the first time in hours that she'd felt good about something. Talking with the cute guy in the mail room had given her the energy to survive the last half hour of the day. It was only as she stepped onto the elevator that she realized she didn't even know his name.

Chapter 4

Maria looked at her watch again. "It's nearly seven o'clock," she said to Enid, who sat across from her in a booth at the Dairi Burger Monday night. "It's not like Liz to be so late."

Enid shrugged. "She had to battle rush-hour traffic out of Los Angeles," she pointed out. "I'm sure she'll be here any minute, as soon as she drops off Jessica."

"I hope Liz doesn't mind that we ordered without her," Maria said as a waiter slid plates full of burgers and fries onto the table.

"Tell me more about the set you're designing for *Evita*," Enid urged.

"I'm not really designing it," Maria said. "Remember, I'm only the student intern. I'm just helping the real set designer. Tell me more about your literary agency."

"My day was fantastic!" Enid replied. "But you tell me about your day first. Doesn't the set for *Evita* call for high-tech stuff like audiovisual screens?"

Maria nodded and sipped her milk shake. "It's going to be so cool—"

Suddenly Enid stood up and waved toward the door. "Elizabeth, over here!" she called. "Maria was just about to tell me about the set she's helping to design for a musical," she continued as Elizabeth approached the booth. Unlike Maria and Enid, Elizabeth was still wearing her work clothes. She slid onto the bench beside Maria.

"Are you ready to order?" the waiter asked. Maria saw Elizabeth glance at the cheeseburgers in front of her friends.

"The chef's salad," Elizabeth decided. "And a diet soda."

Enid raised her eyebrows. "That's not your usual order," she pointed out.

"I know," Elizabeth replied. "But I've been working all day around women who look like they live on celery and rice cakes. I have to watch my calories if I'm going to make it in the fashion industry."

Maria laughed. "Girl, get *over* it! It's only a two-week internship."

"Maybe not," Elizabeth said. "My new boss says I could wrangle a summer job out of this—if I play my cards right."

"That's wonderful, Liz!" Enid said. "You'll have to tell us all about it. But first I want to hear about *Evita*. Go on with what you were saying, Maria."

"For the palace scenes we'll have the palace—the Casa Rosada—on stage left, with the balcony where the actors will stand," Maria explained. "I'll be painting the wall of the building to look like pink marble. Then there will be a huge movie screen . . ." Maria's voice trailed off. "Elizabeth?" she asked. Her friend was staring at a spot on the wall over Enid's shoulder. "Are you OK?"

Elizabeth seemed surprised, as if she'd just been awakened. "Sure, I'm fine," she said, blinking. "Do you think this navy suit is too old-fashioned?"

"Of course not," Enid said. "You only bought it last season." She winked at Maria. "I know—now that you're in the fashion industry, you can't be seen in public wearing last year's suit! Gee, Maria. After one day she's turned into Lila Fowler."

"A fate worse than death!" Maria intoned dramatically.

Elizabeth smiled weakly. "I'm not worried that the suit's from last season. It's the style. I feel frumpy."

"You're not frumpy," Enid assured her. "You're professional-looking."

"You could borrow Jessica's leopard-print bikini

53

to wear to work tomorrow," Maria suggested. "Nobody would call you frumpy then."

"You two are no help," Elizabeth said with a distracted laugh.

"Go on, Maria!" Enid urged. "Tell us more about *Evita*. Speaking of fashion, what are the costumes like?"

"The Rainbow Tour sequence has the most fabulous gowns!" Maria said. "There's this scarlet one with a tight bodice and a full skirt that is totally to die for. Listen to this, Liz. . . . Liz? Oh, *E-liz-a-beth!*" Elizabeth's eyes again were fixed, unblinking, on a spot on the wall. Maria waved her hand in front of her friend's face until Elizabeth emerged from her reverie and shook her head. "What planet are you visiting this evening?" Maria asked, beginning to get annoyed.

"Are you sure there's nothing wrong?" Enid asked, her eyes showing concern.

"I need an emergency shopping trip!" Elizabeth announced, rising to her feet.

"I was right!" Enid said. "She's been Lila-fied!"

"Bummer," replied Maria. "Do you think it's contagious?"

"I'm not kidding, you two!" Elizabeth argued. "My clothes were all wrong today. You should have seen all those women at *Flair*. They looked so stylish and sophisticated. And I looked like a nineteen fifties schoolgirl."

"That's so untrue, Liz," Maria said. "Nobody at

Flair expects you to run out and buy a whole new wardrobe for a two-week internship."

"Besides, what would you buy it *with?*" Enid asked. "You may be developing a Lila attitude, but I doubt her credit cards come with it."

"I'll use some of my savings," Elizabeth replied.

"That," Maria objected, "is the lamest idea you've ever had. I thought you were saving for a new computer."

"I was," Elizabeth said with a shrug. "But I've got this terrific opportunity to jump-start my future career. I can't let a dowdy wardrobe stand in my way."

"Maybe you should give this some more thought," Enid suggested evenly.

"There's no time for that!" Elizabeth protested. "And there's no time for hanging around here arguing about it. I only have two weeks to make a good impression. I can't blow it. I'm going to the mall tonight. *Now!*"

"I thought you were meeting Todd after we finish dinner," Maria reminded her.

"Not until later," Elizabeth said. "I've got time for a shopping spree first if I hurry." She stopped and looked at both her friends. "You two can sit here getting fat—or you can come with me to Valley Mall."

Maria, perplexed, looked at Enid, who shrugged. They threw some money on the table to pay for their meals, and they followed Elizabeth out of the Dairi Burger.

❖　　❖　　❖

Elizabeth sat at Cheveux, a hair salon at Valley Mall, scrutinizing her reflection in the mirror as she described what she wanted to Fifi, the styling specialist.

"*Oui*," Fifi replied. "You want the style *du jour*."

"The style of the day?" Elizabeth asked.

"Every couple of months the beautiful people in L.A. discover a new one," Fifi explained with a shrug. "Right now it's cut long in the front. Next month it might be layered, or snipped short all around, or swept off the face, or teased on top."

In the mirror Elizabeth noticed Enid and Maria exchanging glances. They were sitting in the waiting area, a few steps away, with shopping bags full of Elizabeth's new outfits clustered around them. Obviously her friends thought she was out of her mind to pay a small fortune for a trendy haircut and clothes. But if she needed to revamp her appearance in order to impress Leona Peirson—and get a summer job at *Flair*—then that's exactly what she would do.

She watched in the mirror as Fifi began snipping away at her hair. As the blond tresses fell to the linoleum around her Elizabeth's eyes widened. A new, more sophisticated version of herself was gradually appearing in the mirror.

Fifi pulled out a blow dryer and a bottle of spritzer and began shaping Elizabeth's new style. And the sophisticated Elizabeth in the mirror replaced the old Elizabeth completely.

"That's perfect!" Elizabeth whispered, hardly recognizing herself. "You didn't cut that much off, but what a difference!" With her new hairstyle and her new clothes, she'd be as sophisticated as any of the sleek women who'd ignored her in the elevator that morning. She imagined herself walking into a high-level editorial meeting at *Flair*, as sure of herself as Leona was. Suddenly it wasn't that hard to picture. She turned to her friends. "What do you guys think?"

"Très chic!" Maria said with a whistle.

"You look great, Liz—very stylish," Enid said. She bit her lip. "But have you seen the time? You were supposed to meet Todd fifteen minutes ago."

"Oops," Elizabeth said with a shrug. "I guess he's just going to have to wait."

At ten-thirty that night Jessica sat on a stool in the bathroom that separated her room from Elizabeth's. Her hair was wrapped in a towel, and her blistered feet were submerged in a pan of steamy water. She leaned forward, her face almost against the mirror, to examine her left eyebrow once more. In her hand a pair of tweezers gleamed.

"I'm getting close, Prince Albert!" she announced to the family's golden retriever. Prince Albert lay with his face on his front paws, gazing quizzically at her from the open doorway to her bedroom. "I only have a few more hairs to tweeze away, and my eyebrows will look just like Simone's!"

Prince Albert whined his play-with-me whine.

"Not now, Albert," Jessica told the dog. "This is serious business!"

Jessica was usually the retriever's first choice for a playmate. But that night she was the only choice. The twins' parents were at a party for the partners in Mr. Wakefield's law firm. Their older brother was a student at Sweet Valley University and only came home for an occasional weekend. And Elizabeth was out with Enid and Maria. Or Todd. Jessica couldn't remember which. As for Jessica herself, she'd been too tired after work to do anything except stagger home and vegetate in front of the television until it was time to begin her before-bed beauty routine.

Now she stared at the one offending eyebrow hair that was still out of place. She reached up to pluck it away. Then the doorbell rang downstairs and she jumped, tweezing the wrong hair. "Rats!" she cried. "What mentally challenged bonehead is at the front door at this hour?"

Prince Albert slowly rose to his feet and barked once, his tail wagging.

"Some watchdog you are!" Jessica said. "Couldn't you have barked to warn me—before the doorbell rang?"

She sighed, reluctantly pulled her feet from the soothing water, and hobbled downstairs to answer the door.

"Elizabeth?" she asked, her newly thinned eyebrows arching up her forehead as she opened the door for her twin.

"Sorry," Elizabeth said, noting Jessica's fuzzy pink bathrobe and the towel around her hair. "My hands were too full to reach my keys." She stepped over the threshold and deposited a half-dozen shopping bags on the carpet.

"Wow!" Jessica exclaimed. "You hardly look like us anymore! Your hair is totally awesome!"

"Do you really think so?" Elizabeth asked. "Is it stylish enough for *Flair*?"

"Absolutely," Jessica breathed. "You'll be the talk of the elevator tomorrow. Why didn't you tell me? I'd have gone with you. After work tomorrow I'm going to get mine cut just like it!"

Elizabeth rolled her eyes. "I don't think so," she said, sounding a little snooty. "Do you have any idea what Cheveux charges for a cut like this? There's no way you can afford it—unless you've saved a lot more of your allowance for the past six months than you've let on."

Jessica narrowed her eyes. "You know, Liz," she said. "It's bad enough that I have to deal with a stuck-up brat at *work* for two weeks—"

"*Relax,* Jess," Elizabeth interrupted. "You're just jealous because you still look like a high-school student. I'm sorry. I'm not trying to upstage you. But it's more important for *me* to look stylish."

Jessica crossed her arms menacingly. "And why is that?" she asked in a cold, steady voice.

"I have a chance to turn this internship into a career!" Elizabeth answered. "I'm not talking about a fantasy, like becoming a supermodel. I'm talking about a real summer job as an editorial assistant at *Flair*. But I can't get it if I don't make the right impression."

"You know, Elizabeth," Jessica said icily, "I like your new haircut a whole lot better than I like your new attitude."

With those words, Jessica spun around and stomped back upstairs, her feet stinging with every step.

Chapter 5

Elizabeth felt the other women staring behind her as she stepped out of the elevator on the eleventh floor Tuesday morning. No one had actually complimented her new clothes and hairstyle, but at least she didn't feel invisible.

After the doors closed, she checked her appearance in their mirrored surface. She pursed her plum-colored lips and tried to inspect herself objectively. Her new periwinkle blue ensemble wasn't quite as elegant as some of the ones she'd seen on the elevator that morning. But it was more stylish than anything else she owned, with a short skirt, a fitted vest, and a long, tailored blazer. She knew it suited her.

"Elizabeth, is that you?" exclaimed a voice behind her. She whirled to see Leona appraising her new look. "I'm overwhelmed by the change,"

Leona raved. "Your hair is absolutely fabulous! And the outfit is perfect. That pink blouse really brings out your complexion."

Elizabeth felt as if she'd just passed some secret initiation ritual. "Thanks, Leona," she said as they walked together down the corridor. "I was nervous about trying something so different from my usual chinos and oxford shirts."

"There's nothing wrong with the preppie look for hanging out at home, if that's what you're comfortable in," Leona said. Elizabeth tried, but she couldn't imagine sophisticated Leona in baggy khaki trousers and a button-down shirt—not at home or anywhere. "But a career in fashion publishing requires an up-to-date look," Leona continued, ushering Elizabeth into her office. She motioned to a chair, and Elizabeth sat down.

"I'm glad I went out and bought some new things," Elizabeth began tentatively. "I know I fit in around here much better, dressed this way. But it also bothers me a little—" She stopped, wondering if she was out of line.

"Go on, Elizabeth, please," Leona urged as she poured coffee for both of them. "I told you to be completely honest with me, and I meant it."

Elizabeth plunged ahead. "It's just that I hate to think people will judge me on my appearance instead of on my work," she concluded.

"Every businesswoman dreams of a day

when we're judged solely by the quality of the work we do," the managing editor said thoughtfully. "But the reality is that appearances do count—and much more so for women than for men."

"But that's not fair!" Elizabeth exclaimed.

"No, it's not," Leona agreed. "But to make it in any industry, you have to be a pragmatist. And this industry is extraordinarily competitive. Of course, if you can't do the work, you don't stand a chance. But a lot of women are skilled. Qualifications are a given, and they aren't the deciding factor in success."

"Then what is?" Elizabeth asked, thrilled to be discussing issues of feminism and business with someone as successful as Leona. "You can't mean to tell me that clothes and hair are the only difference between women who get ahead and those who don't."

"Of course not," Leona replied. She took a long sip from her coffee mug. "Image is important. But drive, ambition, and that extra spark of creativity are the things that really count. You have to be willing to take risks, to go out on a limb when necessary."

Elizabeth grimaced. "I'm not sure I'm enough of a risk taker," she confessed. "My twin sister, Jessica, is the one who goes out on limbs—and most of the time they get cut out from under her!"

"I'm talking about *calculated* risks," Leona clarified. "And I think you're wrong about not being a risk taker. You took a big risk today, changing your entire image just because of a comment I made. That took courage."

"Not really—," Elizabeth objected. "It would have taken more courage to keep showing up looking like a schoolgirl."

"Well, it does take courage to be different," Leona admitted. "But in this case being different served no purpose. I'm impressed that you have so much desire to succeed at *Flair* that you would make such a big change, even though you're only guaranteed a two-week run."

Elizabeth smiled shyly. "I do have one confession to make," she said. "I didn't have enough courage to try the gold eye shadow I bought!"

Leona laughed. "Give it two weeks," she joked. "We'll have your eyelids sparkling before you know it. But as long as we're talking about fashion, I'd love your opinion on a new dress I bought last night."

"You have it here?" Elizabeth asked. She felt flattered that Leona was taking the time to talk to her about something personal rather than business related.

"I'm dropping it off for alterations at lunchtime," Leona said, pulling a shopping bag from under her desk. She unfurled a short black dress with a plunging neckline, a body-skimming shape, and suede trim. "It's a Lina Lapin," she explained.

A week earlier Elizabeth would have rolled her eyes if Jessica had raved about such a trendy dress. But one day at *Flair* had left her more open-minded about fashion. Besides, the dress would look terrific on Leona's tall, slim frame. "Very chic," Elizabeth said truthfully.

"You don't think the hemline is too high for me, do you?" Leona asked. "My legs aren't what they were when I was your age."

"Nonsense," Elizabeth replied. "Your legs are perfect. What color hose will you wear with it?" Then she nearly laughed out loud at herself. It was exactly the kind of question Jessica would have asked.

Leona raised her eyebrows. "Black lace," she said dramatically.

Elizabeth remembered the evening fashion spreads she'd seen the day before in recent issues of *Flair.* "Lace is totally in," she told Leona. Elizabeth had noticed some Lina Lapin designs in those magazines; the new dress must have cost Leona a fortune. "But what's the occasion? Are you going somewhere special?"

"I think so," Leona answered, her voice tinged with nervous excitement. "My boyfriend's been hinting that he has something big to discuss with me. I'm almost positive he's going to ask me to marry him. I wanted to be wearing a real knockout dress when he pops the question."

"Congratulations—prematurely, I guess," Elizabeth said, giving her boss a warm grin. "That's fantastic!"

"Apparently I'm not the only one with a love life," Leona said, leaning forward conspiratorially across her desk. "I noticed a photograph of a very handsome young man on your desk yesterday."

"That's my boyfriend, Todd," Elizabeth explained, blushing slightly.

"Is he doing an internship this week as well?" Leona asked.

Elizabeth nodded. "He's working in the executive offices of a software company just this side of Sweet Valley," she replied. "To tell you the truth, he's not too excited about it. But I bet he'll learn a lot anyhow."

"I'd love to meet him," Leona said. "Let me know if he can manage a couple of hours away from the office sometime. Maybe the two of us and our significant others can do lunch."

Elizabeth beamed. She'd been excited yesterday that Leona was taking an interest in her as an employee and protégée. Now it seemed that they were becoming friends too.

Jessica sidled into one of the rooms off the main studio in the photography department. "Oh, hello, Michael," she said to Michael Rietz, the hairstylist, pretending to be surprised to see him. "I didn't realize you were in. It's awfully quiet around here this morning."

"You're not complaining, are you?" Michael asked with an amused grin as he set a row of bottled styling gels and mousses on the counter. "If you like, I could call Quentin out of his meeting with the art director and tell him you need some work to do."

"I wouldn't want to interrupt him," Jessica said with mock seriousness. "He's a very important man."

"If you can hang on for a few hours, Simone will be in around lunchtime," Michael said. "I noticed yesterday how much you enjoy helping her out."

"I enjoy helping her, all right," Jessica replied darkly. "I'd really enjoy helping her out the door!" She had experienced enough of Michael's personality to know he wouldn't be shocked by her lack of reverence for the leggy model. Michael focused his attention on a bottle of setting lotion, but Jessica thought she saw a grin curl the corners of his lips. She stared at herself in the mirror. "You know, Michael," she began tentatively, "I've been thinking about making a change in my own hairstyle. Nothing too drastic—just an update. How do you think my hair would look if I wore it shorter in the back?"

Michael squinted at her thoughtfully before

reaching out and running his hand in a professional manner through the long blond waves that framed her face. "Your hair has enough body to hold the look," he finally decided. "Yes, I think it could be a good style for you."

Jessica grinned. "*You* seem to have some time now," she said. "I mean, it would be good practice for you—"

"And heaven knows I need that," Michael added sarcastically. Jessica silently cursed her choice of words. But Michael didn't seem to mind. He shrugged. "All right. I never could say no to a pretty girl. You can be my first customer of the day."

"You won't regret this, Michael. When I'm a famous model, I'll tell everyone that you helped me get started," Jessica vowed as she hopped into the chair. "You'll be so popular, you can open your own fancy salon and charge two hundred dollars for a haircut!"

"Right," he said. "And how do you plan to become a famous model?"

Jessica reached into her backpack and pulled out the scrapbook she'd made with all the best photos of herself. "With *this*," she said. "Here, let me show you how photogenic I am." She handed him the album, opened to a spread of photographs of herself in her Sweet Valley High cheerleading uniform. After giving him enough time to admire the snapshots, she flipped the page to a photograph of her standing on the beach in an aqua bathing suit with a daring neckline and high-cut legs. Then she turned to see how impressed he was. Instead Michael snickered.

Jessica felt rage boiling up inside her. "What's wrong?" she asked hotly as the stylist laid the album on the counter, pulled out a smock, and tied it around her neck. "I think I look great in those pictures. So does everyone else who's seen them!"

Michael shook his head, grinning broadly. "You're a beautiful girl," he said. "But the photographs look as if someone took them with a disposable camera. The exposures are all wrong, you've got shadows on your face, and the colors are murky." He turned her chair and reclined it so he could wet down her hair in the sink. "Sorry to break the news, Jessica. But that album would get you laughed out of any modeling agency in California."

"But *why?*" Jessica demanded as he wrapped a towel around her head. "I want to be a *model*—not a photographer!"

"Modeling's very competitive," Michael replied with a shrug. "There are a lot of pretty girls around. Nobody wants to waste time on one who doesn't present herself as a professional."

"You think I'm too unprofessional to be a model?" Jessica asked, stricken.

"It has nothing to do with what you are. It's all *image*," the stylist answered as he whirled her chair to face the mirror again. "A professional-looking portfolio is everything," he continued. "Get yourself a state-of-the-art camera, find somebody who knows how to use it, and put together a portfolio that looks like you mean business."

"But I can't *afford* a state-of-the-art camera until I start making money as a model!" Jessica wailed.

Michael selected a pair of scissors and began snipping away at Jessica's hair. "The only people who make it in this business are the ones who take risks," he said. "If you're not willing to go all out to achieve your goals . . . well, you'd better get used to running downstairs every half hour to fetch Simone's fancy Swiss mineral water."

"*French* mineral water," Jessica put in. But her mind was working feverishly to come up with a plan for getting her hands on an expensive camera. She was a risk taker. And she was determined to become a model before the internship was over. It shouldn't be too difficult to figure out how.

"So how many of the editors came here from New York when the magazine moved a few months ago?" Elizabeth asked during lunchtime on Tuesday, leaning eagerly across

70

the table at the Mission Café, next door to the Mode building.

"About half," Reggie confided. "Me included. I'm sure the turnover helped get me my promotion to assistant fashion editor. The others didn't want to relocate."

"Beyond the move, what kind of a record does the magazine have for promoting people from within?" Elizabeth asked, twirling a few strands of pasta with her fork.

Reggie shrugged. "I don't pay much attention to things like that, but it seems pretty good. Warren, the guy whose office you're borrowing, was promoted from features assistant to features associate last year."

"I'm still a little hazy on the difference in responsibilities between assistant editor and associate editor," Elizabeth said. "And for that matter, between editorial assistant and assistant editor. What—"

"You are just too much!" Reggie broke in, laughing. "All these questions! It's like you're planning a whole career, not just a two-week internship."

Elizabeth shrugged, but she forced a smile. "I guess I *am* planning a career—or at least exploring the possibilities for one. I mean, isn't that what an internship is for?"

"I wouldn't know," Reggie said. "I never had the guts to apply for this kind of internship when I was sixteen. It's a cutthroat field. But you've sure got the ambition to succeed. I bet the dragon lady loves that!"

"Dragon lady?" Elizabeth asked. "Who are you talking about?"

"Leona Peirson, of course," Reggie replied.

"Leona?" Elizabeth repeated, amazed. "You can't mean that. I think she's terrific! Have you had a problem with her?"

"She really knows her stuff," Reggie admitted. "And no, I haven't exactly had a problem with her. I think it's just that our styles are different. Leona is about the most focused person I've ever met. And she's so aggressive. She intimidates me."

"That's the way a woman has to be if she wants to get ahead," Elizabeth told her new friend.

"I guess you're right," Reggie said. "And I'm not at all like that. I could never be like Leona."

"What are your ambitions, Reggie?" Elizabeth asked. She'd learned enough about Reggie's work to know that the young woman was a top-notch proofreader. Elizabeth knew it was too early to worry, but she couldn't help thinking that Reggie could be tough competition if Elizabeth were ever a full-time employee at *Flair*.

Reggie shook her head slowly and took a sip of her diet soda before replying. "I used to think I wanted a job like Leona's," she said. "But I've been at *Flair* long enough to realize I'm not cut out for it."

"I've heard you're the best proofreader on the staff," Elizabeth said.

"Thanks," Reggie said with a grateful smile. "It's nice to know some people think so. I like my job, and I take pride in my work. But I'm a detail-oriented person, not a big-picture type like Leona."

"You could learn to be," Elizabeth pointed out.

"Maybe," Reggie agreed. "But it's more than that. Getting to the top takes a lot of commitment and sacrifice. I've seen how hard the top editors work, and I can't see myself putting everything else on hold."

Elizabeth grinned. "You mean you want to have a *life* too?"

"Exactly," Reggie replied. "I'd like to get married someday, have a couple of kids, and maybe work part-time while they're babies. Publishing's a pretty good business for that—but only if you're not worried about getting ahead."

"You want to stay in your current job for your whole career?" Elizabeth asked. "Wouldn't you get bored?"

"Maybe not my *current* job," Reggie admitted. "I'd like to move up to associate editor, like Warren. But I'm not ambitious enough to set my sights any higher than that."

"That sounds very sensible," Elizabeth said,

trying to keep the relief out of her voice. She mentally crossed Reggie's name off her mental list of the competition for future jobs at *Flair*.

Jessica glided into the cafeteria of the Mode building during lunchtime on Tuesday, hips thrust forward in her best imitation of Simone's walk. It was easy to feel sophisticated with her stylish new haircut and her fitted purple blazer that was longer than her black leather miniskirt.

"Great hair!" Shelly called, breezing by on her way out of the room. "Quite modern."

Jessica grinned a very un-Simone-like grin. "Thanks," she said. "Michael whipped it up for me this morning. Aren't you going in the wrong direction?"

"I ate early," the makeup artist said. "I have to pick up some cosmetics for this afternoon's shoot so I can make Simone look properly disgusted with life. I wonder when we all decided that models should be snarly."

"Probably when somebody noticed their personalities," Jessica said. "Not that I wouldn't like a chance to abuse the people who've been rotten to me over the years."

"Wouldn't we all?" Shelly replied with a smile.

"Have you seen my sister in here?" Jessica asked.

Shelly shook her head, and the beads in her braids jingled. "I wouldn't know if I had," she pointed out. "Remember, I haven't the faintest idea what your sister looks like."

"Actually you know *exactly* what she looks like," Jessica explained with amusement. "She looks like a clone of me, only more boring. We even have the same hairdo now. Except that hers cost a fortune, and mine was free!"

"Identical twins?" Shelly asked. "That's wild! But nope, I haven't seen anyone who looks like you." She checked the clock on the wall. "Sorry," she said. "Gotta run. You know how the fashion goddess gets if you keep her waiting!"

Jessica proceeded toward the cafeteria line, digging in her backpack for her wallet. It wasn't there.

"Rats!" she cried, blushing when she noticed several sophisticated, carefully groomed women turning to stare at her. She silently chastised herself. Fashion models didn't say things like "rats." Suddenly she had a perfectly clear vision of her wallet, sitting on the kitchen counter at home, where she'd set it down that morning. Without it she was flat broke.

She scrambled to the telephone in the lobby, completely forgetting to walk like Simone, and dialed Elizabeth's department.

"Come on, Liz," she said aloud. "Answer your phone. You always have a few extra dollars to lend me." When Elizabeth didn't answer, the call was switched to the department's administrative assistant, who said Elizabeth had left for lunch a half hour earlier.

"Rats!" Jessica yelled again, turning the stylishly coiffed heads of several women who were waiting near the elevator.

Oh, well, Jessica told herself. If people were going to stare at her, at least they would see her chic new hairstyle. She was hungry, but she couldn't do much about that with no money. She'd noticed a courtyard between the Mode building and the high-rise next door. It seemed like the perfect place to give people a chance to compliment her on her new hairstyle as she worked on her suntan.

A few minutes later she was lounging on a concrete bench, with her sunglasses on and her eyes closed. The sun felt deliciously warm on her face and arms, and her hair slid lightly and stylishly against her shoulders. She tried to concentrate on the sun and on the fabulous photo opportunity she was providing for any passing shutterbugs. But it was no use. Her stomach was growling so loudly, she didn't know how she would survive until dinnertime.

"Uh-oh," said a sexy voice nearby. "It's Sleeping Beauty again. Do I dare kiss you in front of all these people?"

Jessica opened her eyes and raised the sunglasses to her forehead. The mail-room hunk from the day before was standing over her. "Would that cause a big enough scandal to get my photograph in *Flair* magazine?" she asked him.

"Would you settle for the *National Inquisitor*?" he replied, looking even more sexy than he had yesterday. The sunlight brought out a golden twinkle in his deep brown eyes that Jessica found mesmerizing.

Jessica shaded her eyes with one hand as she pretended to consider his question. "Nah," she decided. "I've been in trashy tabloids before. There's no future in it."

"Then I guess I'll have to restrain myself," the guy said, sitting on the edge of the bench. "It'll take all the willpower I've got, though. Do you have any idea how great you look in that short skirt, with your hair shining in the sun?"

"Yes," Jessica replied truthfully, bending one knee in order to show off her toned, tanned leg. "But I wouldn't mind hearing it again."

"You look gorgeous—much better than any slinky fashion model Quentin Berg has ever photographed," he told her. "But at the same time you seem kind of sad. Are you trying to imitate the famous Simone I'm-so-bored-with-life frown? Or is something wrong?"

Jessica swung her legs around so that she was sitting beside him. "I'll say!" she replied. "I was a total space cadet this morning and left my wallet with all my money at home. My sister seems to be off power-lunching with some publishing tycoon, so I'm stuck with nothing to eat."

"Bummer," the guy sympathized. "But that's easy enough to fix." He pulled a paper bag from his backpack. "You can power-lunch with me! How does half a tuna sandwich sound?"

"Terrific," Jessica replied gratefully.

"Also on the menu today at Chez Bench we have a lovely half bag of potato chips, sliced thin and cooked to order with a delicate sheen of grease," the guy said as he unpacked the rest of his lunch. "The house wine is a diet cherry cola, aged to perfection. And on the dessert menu the specialty of the day is Oreo cookies."

"This is terribly, terribly embarrassing," Jessica said, picking up on his fake-posh accent. "But with whom do I have the pleasure of eating?"

"Your charming luncheon companion is Mr. Cameron Smith," the guy replied with a slight bow.

"And I'm Jessica Wakefield," she introduced herself after swallowing her first bite of sandwich.

"Oh, but your fame has preceded you," Cameron said, gesturing with a potato chip. "I know your name, and I know you're the photography intern—or *slave*, as you put it yesterday. I even know that you live in Sweet Valley and have a twin sister who's in editorial."

"How do you know so much about me?" Jessica demanded.

Cameron smiled mysteriously. "We mail-room

guys know everything about everyone," he said with a vaguely European accent.

Did you have to remind me about your job? Jessica almost asked aloud. For a few minutes Cameron's thoughtfulness, good looks, and obvious admiration for her had made Jessica forget that he was a lowly mail-room worker. Now, looking into his laughing brown eyes as he began telling funny stories about *Flair* staff members, she forced herself to remember that she wasn't interested in him. Cameron was smart without being nerdy and nice without being boring. He was funny and warm and full of life—and an undeniable hunk. But he was a nobody.

She had to keep her sights set on Quentin. Of course, the photographer was a jerk and a control freak. But he was a jerk and a control freak who could make her career.

"So when are you going to give me the chance to regale you with more of my scintillating stories?" Cameron asked, breaking into her thoughts.

Jessica smiled. "Oh, I'm sure we'll see each other around," she said evasively, reminding herself again, more sternly this time, that she wasn't interested in Cameron.

"I get it," Cameron said. "I'm talking too much. But next time I'll show you what a great listener I can be. Just try me. You know, I'm dying to hear the story behind that remark you made earlier about being in the trashy tabloids." He paused and looked away momentarily. When he glanced back at Jessica, a faint blush colored his cheeks, and his deep brown eyes looked nervous. "How about if you let me take you to dinner tomorrow night and you can tell me all about it?" he asked in a rush.

Even though his adorable shyness sent a warm tingle right up Jessica's arms, she lied, "I'm, uh, *busy* tomorrow night."

"I know, you're worried about the menu," Cameron pressed on. "I promise you can have a whole sandwich to yourself next time. Maybe even french fries!"

"That's tempting," Jessica said. "But I really can't. You know, I'm so tired by the time I get home from work. And I have a long commute in the morning—"

"Friday night it is!" Cameron exclaimed. "You can play Sleeping Beauty again all Saturday morning."

"Thanks, Cameron," Jessica said, "but I really can't."

Cameron examined her carefully, obviously disappointed. "Does this have anything to do with the fact that I work in the mail room?" he asked, unable to keep a hurt tone from creeping into his voice.

"Of course not!" Jessica replied quickly. "I just—"

"Don't make excuses," Cameron said quietly. "I

get it. And I'm really sorry you feel that way. I was beginning to like you a lot."

"Me too," Jessica whispered under her breath as Cameron abruptly stood up and walked away. But she was sure she had done the right thing. To succeed in the fashion industry, she had to stay focused. She had to create careful alliances and make hard sacrifices.

Still, she felt curiously deflated as Cameron disappeared into the Mode building.

Elizabeth pulled out her wallet to pay her half of the bill at the Mission Café. Then she froze. One of the most handsome men she'd ever seen was walking across the pink-and-gray dining room, wearing an expensively cut suit and a narrow, multicolored tie. He was tall, at least six-foot four, with longish brown hair, bright blue eyes, and chiseled features.

Across the table Reggie sighed audibly, her black eyes following him across the room. "Isn't he beautiful?" Reggie asked in a breathless whisper.

"Who is he?" Elizabeth asked. "Do you know him?"

Reggie shrugged, still watching the man. The waiter was seating him at a table near the window, where a distinguished, silver-haired man was already sipping a glass of wine. "I wouldn't say that I know him exactly," Reggie confessed, more flustered than Elizabeth had seen her before. "I mean, I've had a big, big crush on him ever since I was introduced to him at an office party. But I'm sure he doesn't have the slightest recollection of me."

"An office party?" Elizabeth asked. "He works for *Flair?*"

"He is *Flair*," Reggie replied dreamily. "Don't you recognize him? That's Gordon Lewis, the hotshot new publisher."

"That's Gordon Lewis?" Elizabeth asked. "The Gordon Lewis who brought *Flair* to Los Angeles?"

"The one and only," Reggie said. "All the New York publishing snobs said it couldn't be done, but he was determined to start a new center for fashion publishing on the West Coast."

"I was expecting him to be older," Elizabeth marveled. "He can't be more than twenty-eight!"

"Something like that," Reggie said, her eyes still glued to the tall, handsome publisher.

"Who's the man with him?" Elizabeth said. "Should I recognize him?"

Reggie shook her head. "I don't know. Probably a big-time advertiser—president of a cosmetics firm or something. Who cares? Gordon Lewis is much more interesting."

Elizabeth agreed, but for different reasons. Reggie was right: Gordon Lewis was astonishingly good-looking. But Elizabeth's interest in the publisher was mostly professional. She memorized every detail of his face and tried to remember everything she'd ever read about him. Here was a man who could help her go places. Elizabeth vowed that before her internship was through, Gordon Lewis would know her name.

Chapter 6

Jessica hurried into the photo studio, hoping nobody would notice she was ten minutes late returning from lunch. Quentin was busy harassing two carpenters who were building something that looked like a giant sandbox on one end of the room. On the couch in the corner reclined Simone, chomping on a stalk of celery. As Jessica walked by she spoke.

"It must be difficult, having such a terrible weight problem," Simone observed, looking Jessica up and down.

Jessica trembled with rage. But she clamped her mouth shut before a barrage of insults spilled out. Quentin was nearby; she couldn't risk having him listen in while she broke the Toothpick into kindling. *But someday—soon—I'll put that twig in her place,* she swore to herself. Taking over

Simone's modeling job was no longer a desire. It was a *necessity*.

Todd aligned his hundredth document of the day against the inch marks on the glass surface of the photocopying machine. For the hundredth time of the day he cursed himself for being stuck at Varitronics while Aaron was assisting the manager of the L.A. Lakers. To make matters worse, he'd spent the whole day doing routine office work for Margaret Meeks, who reminded him more of a drill sergeant than an administrative assistant. He jabbed the green copy button on the top of the machine and waited for the all-too-familiar whirring sound that meant the invoice was being copied. Instead the machine beeped twice. Then silence.

The greenish electronic display line on the front of the machine announced Out of Paper. Todd gritted his teeth. He pounded one fist on the top of the machine—but not nearly as hard as he wanted to hit it. Then he sighed and dropped to his knees to open the front panel.

"What do you mean, out of paper?" he asked the machine, grateful that nobody was near enough to hear him talking to a pile of metal. "There's a whole *stack* of paper in there!"

He slammed the panel closed, pressed the clear button, and hit the copy button again.

Close Panel Door, the machine's display demanded.

"I closed it!" he hissed back. "The door is closed. You've got paper. What more do you want?" Sighing again, he wrenched the door open and slammed it, harder.

Out of Paper, the machine complained.

"Try switching it off," called a junior staff member who was walking by, trying to hide a grin. "Turn it back on after thirty seconds, and it might decide to cooperate."

Todd punched the off button with his thumb. Then he waited thirty seconds, staring at his watch and wishing it were later than two-thirty in the afternoon. He switched the machine back on, waited for it to warm up, and then pressed the copy button again.

The machine whirred obediently and then stopped. Out of Toner, the display announced.

"You are *not* out of toner," Todd said to the machine through clenched lips. "I fed you a new cartridge just this morning."

Out of Toner, the machine blinked.

Todd wrenched open the door on the front panel, exposed the toner cartridge, and slammed it with the heel of his hand to make sure it was in place. A cloud of black powder erupted from the cartridge and quickly settled all over his suit, his white shirt, and the elegant dove gray carpeting.

"That's *it!*" he announced. "I can't take another second of this place." His father and most of the managers were tied up in a meeting that was

87

expected to last until dinnertime. And Meeks was in the accounting department, arguing about some invoices. If he was lucky, nobody would even notice if he cut out early. He would drive into the city and surprise Elizabeth by picking her up at the magazine.

Todd shut the front panel of the photocopying machine. Then he sauntered back to his own cubicle, ceremoniously loosening his tie and tossing it onto his workstation. As he passed Meeks's empty desk and made for the door he shrugged out of his blazer and unfastened the top button of his shirt. *Free at last,* he thought happily.

Jessica slipped into a small photo studio that was empty except for a few camera bags and some photographic equipment lying on a desk. She picked up the telephone and punched in the number for Fowler Enterprises.

"Fowler Enterprises," growled Lila. "May I help you?"

"You sound like you're transmitting death rays through the telephone with your voice," Jessica observed. "You make about as good a receptionist as I do a common laborer."

"Well, greetings to you too," Lila seethed. "Honestly, Jess, I'd love to transmit death rays to the dweeb who dreamed up these internships. Lila Fowler—millionaire, world traveler, best-dressed girl in southern California, and *telephone lackey?*

Do you know that they expect me to be *nice* to everyone who calls here? They've absolutely *got* to be kidding."

"Nobody cares if I'm nice," Jessica said. "I could be a robot. I'm just supposed to keep my mouth shut and take orders."

"I am *not* an *answering machine!*" Lila declared. "This whole thing is just too surreal."

"Yeah, well, I'm learning all about surreal," Jessica said, eyeing Quentin and Simone through the open door to the main studio. "Right now Simone is refusing to pose—it seems that her mineral water is from the wrong country! And Quentin, who's Mr. Control Freak when it comes to ordering me around, is telling the poor girl how brave she is to continue in the face of such disaster. Lila, I swear I'm going to be sick!"

"Spare me the whining, Jessica," Lila said. "At least you're somewhere glamorous. I mean, I knew my father made computer chips for a living, but nobody here can talk about anything else! Can you imagine anything so boring?"

"Don't mention chips," Jessica begged. "I only had half a lunch today. I'm dying of starvation!"

"And I just broke a fingernail on this idiotic switchboard," Lila said. "My father is definitely going to hear about this!"

"Li, listen to me," Jessica said. "This is an emergency. I need you to meet me at the beach after work today."

"The beach?" Lila asked. "What kind of emergency is this?"

Jessica glanced through the door toward Quentin and the Toothpick. "I can't talk about it now. Just meet me at the beach."

"But why—?"

"Don't ask questions," Jessica ordered. "Just do it. Oh, and bring those new sunglasses you bought at the mall Sunday—the retro ones with the rhinestones. And your purple headband. And your makeup kit."

"Jessica—"

"Please, Lila!" Jessica begged. "I'll explain everything when I see you tonight."

After she hung up the phone, Jessica glanced back into the main studio, where Simone was finally stepping into the enormous sandbox that was supposed to make the photographs look as if they'd been shot on a stylized beach. She waited until all eyes were upon her. Then she slowly unwrapped her silk robe to expose one of the tiniest bikinis Jessica had ever seen.

"Spectacular, honey!" Quentin called as he snapped photograph after photograph. "Now take a step to the left. I want to get the beach umbrella in the shot . . . and let the robe fall behind you so I can see every bit of that bathing suit . . . perfect!"

Jessica slitted her eyes and clenched her jaw. As far as she was concerned, Simone looked as appealing as a praying mantis—she was certainly

as skinny as one. *Come to think of it,* Jessica remembered, *don't female praying mantises eat the
heads off their mates? It would serve Quentin
right, the way he's carrying on over that six-foot
toothpick.*

But Jessica needed Quentin. He was her ticket
to fame and fortune. First, though, she needed a
professional portfolio. And for that she needed
professional equipment. She eyed one of Quentin's
spare cameras, lying out on the desk. Did she dare
borrow it for the night?

Suddenly Michael Rietz's voice echoed in her
head. *The only people who make it in this business
are the ones who take risks.* If she wasn't willing to
go all out to achieve her goals, the stylist had said,
then she'd better get used to fetching Simone's
mineral water.

"That's not going to happen," Jessica said aloud
with determination. She glanced through the doorway again. Nobody was paying her the slightest bit
of attention. There were advantages to being invisible. *Quentin has more cameras than Lila has
bathing suits,* Jessica rationalized. He'd never miss
this one. Would he? Besides, it was only for one
night.

She stuffed the camera in her backpack and
zipped it up.

Elizabeth clicked the mouse button to maneu-
ver through cyberspace to the Library of Congress

91

database. As a subject heading she punched in the name of a chemical found in certain sunscreens. Leona was writing an article on studies that had shown the chemical to cause breathing difficulties, and Elizabeth was glad to help research a topic more important than how to color-coordinate accessories.

"You're beautiful when you're surfing the Net," said a voice from her doorway. Elizabeth looked up, startled. Todd was lounging against the door of her office, smiling at her. He wore a distinctly unprofessional outfit: a Sweet Valley University T-shirt and a pair of cutoff shorts.

"What are you doing here?" she asked.

"Bringing you coffee," he replied, setting a steaming cup beside her keyboard.

"You came an awfully long way to bring me a cup of coffee," Elizabeth noted, turning back to the screen to narrow her search parameters.

"That's OK. It's really awful coffee," he explained. "But I know you professional journalists drink it black and bitter."

Elizabeth gulped a mouthful. "You're right on both counts," she said. "It's awful, and everyone around here does drink it black. But it's just what I needed. Thanks." She tilted her face up to accept a kiss.

"So how about you knock off a little early here and let me take you home?" Todd asked, rubbing her aching shoulders.

"Mmmm," Elizabeth murmured. "That sounds great. And it feels great. But I can't. I have to compile a bibliography for Leona before I leave here tonight." She looked down at her watch. "Todd, it's only four o'clock! You're supposed to be at Varitronics! Wearing a suit!"

Todd shrugged. "I got sick of fighting with the copying machine, so I gave myself the rest of the afternoon off," he admitted. "I changed into the most un-Varitronics outfit I could find, and here I am. It's about time I saw your office."

"What do you think?" Elizabeth asked, peering at her monitor to check on the progress of her search.

"Pretty classy digs you've got here at *Flair*," Todd said, nodding. "Your own office! With a door and everything. At Varitronics I have to fold myself into a cubicle about the size of my gym locker."

"So much for being the boss's son," Elizabeth noted. "Didn't anyone care that you decided to bag the rest of the day?"

"I wouldn't know," Todd replied. "I didn't tell anyone. I bet you could do the same thing—just slip out of here with me without anyone knowing."

Elizabeth shook her head. "Maybe I *could*, but I won't," she said. "I promised Leona I'd finish this tonight."

"Come on, Liz!" Todd urged. "Just this once. She'll understand."

"I've got too much to do," Elizabeth told him

firmly. "It's not just this bibliography. I could stay all night and not finish everything."

"Well, *sorry*," Todd said, his voice sounding hurt. "I thought you'd be happy to see me."

Elizabeth smiled apologetically. "I *am* happy to see you," she said soothingly. "And I know you drove all the way from Sweet Valley to pick me up. But I can't just blow off the rest of this work. You know it's important for me to make a good impression in this internship. My future career may depend on it!"

"OK," Todd said, massaging her shoulders again. "I understand. And I did agree to share you with the publishing world for two weeks. So I'll just sit here and watch you. Maybe I can even help you finish sooner."

"That won't work," Elizabeth objected. "There's only one computer. And I can't concentrate with you right behind me." She thought for a moment. "I have an idea. Why don't you go down to the photo studio and visit Jessica? I'm sure she'd love a distraction."

Todd's mouth twisted as if he'd eaten something sour. "Visit *Jessica*?" he asked. "You said this internship might require some sacrifices, but isn't that a little extreme? When was the last time I voluntarily hung out with your psycho twin?"

"I know she's not your favorite person," Elizabeth said, smiling up at her boyfriend. "But watching somebody type must be even more frustrating than wrestling with a photocopying machine. Jessica's working in a photography studio. There must be props and colorful sets and clothes down there, with photographers running all around. It's got to be more exciting than this." She gestured with her hand at the piles of paper on her desk.

Todd sighed. "If I go down to see Jessica for twenty minutes, do you promise you'll let me take you away from all this afterward?"

"Make it thirty minutes, and you've got a deal," Elizabeth told him, relenting. "I think I can finish this bibliography in a half hour."

"Thirty minutes it is," Todd agreed. "Do you promise you won't change your mind and beg to stay longer when I come back up here for you?"

"Scout's honor!" Elizabeth promised. "I came in early this morning, so Leona won't mind if I leave a little early—if I take the 'Fashion Flops' section home with me to proofread tonight."

"You're a total grind," he said fondly.

"It's not being a grind," Elizabeth corrected. "It's *career planning!*"

"Whatever it is, I'm not sure I like it," Todd admitted. "But I guess I'll live." He leaned in to kiss the tip of her nose, but Elizabeth ducked.

"Go, Todd!" she ordered, already staring back at the screen. "The art department is on the ninth floor."

"I don't even get another kiss?" Todd asked.

"In a half hour," Elizabeth promised, fingers already clicking again on the keyboard.

Todd muttered something as he trudged out the door, but Elizabeth was too intent on her work to pay attention.

Chapter 7

Jessica wiped a strand of sweaty, sand-streaked hair out of her eyes. She was grateful that she couldn't see what her stylish new hairdo looked like after a half hour of hard labor under Quentin's white-hot lights.

"*No*, Jessica!" he barked. "I want the sand dune on the *left* to be higher than the one on the *right*."

Jessica motioned to the left with her push broom. "It *is* higher!" she insisted, facing him defiantly.

"Not *your* left!" Quentin chastised her. "*My* left!"

"You could have said so before I swept all that sand around!" she pointed out, trying not to lose her temper with the one person who could make or break her career.

"Just do it like I said and stop arguing,"

Quentin ordered. He turned to consult with the set decorator about the painted backdrop. As soon as he wasn't looking, Jessica turned her back on him long enough to make a bug-eyed face at Shelly, who was touching up Simone's makeup.

"Jessica!" Simone called sharply. "When you're through playing in the sand, I expect you to fetch me that mineral water I asked for ten minutes ago. You have no idea how dehydrating it is, posing under those bright lights." In her white macramé bikini Simone looked as cool as an icicle.

Jessica bit her lip to keep from shrieking. "You're right," she muttered under her breath. "I have no idea what it's like posing under the bright lights. All I know is what it's like *pushing three tons of sand* under the bright lights. I've never been so sweaty and sandy and gross in my entire *life*."

"Did you say something?" Quentin asked sharply.

"Not a thing," Jessica replied sweetly. She had sand in her shoes, sand in her clothes, and sand in her eyes and hair. She could even taste sand in her mouth, crunching between her teeth. *It's a good thing nobody I know can see me like this,* she thought, wondering if the sand was making her eyes bloodshot.

Suddenly Jessica noticed through her gritty eyes that a guy was standing in the doorway, staring at her. And he appeared to be a real hunk. She rubbed furiously at her eyes until she could see clearly.

"Todd?" she exclaimed weakly. She wasn't sure if she should be glad he wasn't a cute guy she cared about impressing or horrified that he was someone who could tell all her friends just how glamorous her internship really was.

"Jessica?" he asked, his eyes widening. "You look, uh . . . *different*."

Quentin was also staring at Todd, Jessica noticed. And the photographer had a strange look on his face, as if he had never seen a teenage guy before.

Uh-oh, Jessica thought. *Todd's about to get thrown out of Quentin's studio!*

For a moment Todd couldn't tear his eyes away from Jessica's forlorn figure. She stood in the middle of some sort of sandbox that took up nearly a quarter of the huge studio, pushing sand around with a broom. She wore a long purple blazer and a short black skirt, but both were spotted with sand. Her eyes were red, she had sand in her hair, and sweaty trails of makeup ran down her face. Her expression was furious in stark contrast to the bright, cheerful beach scene painted in bold strokes of blue and gold on the backdrop behind her.

Todd couldn't decide which was more amazing—the sight of Jessica looking terrible or the sight of Jessica pushing a broom.

He didn't wonder for long. Standing beside the sandbox was one of the best-looking girls he had ever seen. And she was wearing a tantalizingly small bikini made of some sort of white knotted string. As soon as the tall, black-haired beauty turned toward him Todd forgot that Jessica was in the room. With a start he realized that he'd seen the leggy goddess before, on the cover of magazines in the grocery store. She giggled, and Todd blushed. He hadn't meant to stare, especially at that slim, perfectly formed body.

A man's laugh interrupted Todd's stunned daze. Painfully he shifted his gaze away from the breathtaking model. For the first time he noticed the man who was obviously in charge. He was in his midtwenties, with scruffy blond hair, and he stood behind a camera that had as many buttons as a flight simulator, mounted on a tripod. Another camera hung around his neck.

"I'm Quentin Berg, the photographer," the man barked, as if he expected Todd to have heard of him. He didn't sound unkind, but he did sound as if he was used to immediate respect. "And this," he said, gesturing toward the model, "is Simone, wearing the latest Rafael Bartucci design."

"Um, I'm—uh—Todd Wilkins," Todd stammered. "I'm sorry if I interrupted. I can leave if—"

"Have you ever done any modeling?" the photographer asked, studying his face and body in a way that made Todd want to run and hide.

Todd shook his head. "No," he choked out.

"There's no time like the present," Quentin decided. "You've got a look—classic, but hip. Clean-cut, but full of life. I can make it work."

"Do you want me to make him up?" asked an African American woman who stood near Simone at a table covered with tubes and jars of cosmetics.

"Not now, Shelly," Quentin decided. "We've got a male model coming tomorrow to pose on this set with Simone. For now we'll just use Todd as a stand-in for some test shots. But take a look at his features under the lights and decide what you'd do with his coloring. Nothing heavy; keep it natural. If this session works out, I might want to use him on the second Bartucci shoot."

"Are you finished with those sand dunes, Jessica?" Simone asked impatiently. "I'm still waiting for my mineral water."

"Yes, ma'am," Jessica replied, saluting. Simone grunted acknowledgment, but Todd knew Jessica well enough to recognize the wrath in her bloodshot eyes. Jessica stomped into an adjoining room and appeared a moment later with a bottle. She handed it to the taller girl. "Here you are," she said with syrupy, un-Jessica-like sweetness. "French mineral water. I brought a whole stash up here so I don't have to make you wait every time."

Todd didn't understand the surprise he saw on Simone's face or the triumph on Jessica's. But he didn't have long to ponder it.

"Take off your shoes and step onto the sand," Quentin instructed him. "Simone, I'll want you next to Todd, on his right. Todd, put your arm around her waist."

Todd gulped, his mind racing. If Simone hadn't been standing there in that tiny little bikini, he'd have scoffed at the whole idea. He'd always thought modeling was for vain airheads. But one look at Simone left him practically speechless. He allowed himself to be moved into position beside her. When Simone, smiling, lifted his hand and placed it on her right hip, Todd let it rest there. Her skin felt cool and silky smooth under his hand. A curtain of black hair rustled against his shoulder, as soft as a caress.

Todd's heart was pounding in his chest. He was terrified. He was embarrassed. And he couldn't believe his good luck.

"Earth to Liz!" called a voice.

Elizabeth looked up from her computer after sending the results of her latest database search to the printer. She blinked, realizing she'd been staring at the screen for a long, long time. Reggie was standing in the doorway.

"You're working too hard," Reggie told her. "I just wanted to say good night. It's five-thirty, and I'm *outta* here!"

"Five-thirty!" Elizabeth exclaimed. "How did it get to be five-thirty?"

"I couldn't say," Reggie joked. "I hear it happens every night at around this time."

"Todd," Elizabeth said, suddenly remembering the deal she'd made with him.

"No, it's Reggie," Reggie corrected. "Am I missing something here? Or are you suffering from the dreaded Computer Daze Disease?"

"I guess I am," Elizabeth admitted. "My boyfriend, Todd, came by to pick me up a while ago. I made him go down to the photography studio to visit my sister so I could finish this research. But I expected him back here an hour ago."

"Maybe he's having fun down there and lost track of the time," Reggie suggested. "Hanging out around photo shoots is a much more exciting spectator sport than watching us edit."

"That's what I told him," Elizabeth agreed, switching off her computer and scouting around the office for a file she needed to take home. "But Todd has a very low tolerance for hanging out with my 'psycho twin,' as he calls her."

"He'll survive," Reggie assured her.

Elizabeth threw the "Fashion Flops" file into her leather briefcase and headed into the hallway with Reggie. "I feel bad about abandoning him with Jessica," she confided as they stepped onto the elevator. "The poor guy must be out of his mind with boredom."

✧   ✧   ✧

To his surprise, Todd was loving every minute of having his photo taken. It didn't hurt that Simone was gorgeous and was wearing practically nothing. And it especially didn't hurt to have her wrap her arms around him and hold her body close against his. Underfoot, the sand was as soft and warm beneath the bright lights as if he really was at the beach.

"Now turn to the other side!" Quentin called. "Let me see that profile. . . . Todd, you're a natural! I've never seen anyone take to modeling so quickly!"

Todd grinned. He'd never understood Jessica's fascination with modeling. But maybe she was right, for once in her life. Maybe there really was something to this modeling gig. For some reason she was staring at him with venom in her bloodshot eyes. Todd couldn't think of anything he'd done to annoy her. But with Jessica, you never knew. He decided not to worry about it. Whatever his offense was, she'd have forgotten it herself in an hour.

"Take a step forward, Todd," Quentin instructed. "Put both arms around Simone. . . . Yes, just like that! Hold it for a second. This is going to be fantastic! You've got a real future in this business."

Todd dreamed of walking into Varitronics the next morning, throwing his tie on his father's desk—no, scratch that. He dreamed of using his tie to throttle the psychotic photocopying machine. Then he would announce to his dad and the rest of the staff that he'd found a new internship. And by the way, they could see his work on the cover of next month's issue of *Flair*.

Even Aaron would be jealous.

Jessica pursed her lips as she watched Todd strut and preen in front of the camera. "He looks like an overgrown peacock with mousy brown hair," she whispered to Shelly.

Shelly shrugged. "I don't know," she said. "I think he's a hunk."

"Believe me, I've known Todd for years," Jessica said. "He may look like a hunk, but he's got the least hunky personality you can imagine. When he has any personality at all. I can't believe he's making a total fool of himself the first time anyone with a camera shows interest."

"Quentin's not the only one showing interest," Shelly whispered back.

"That's for sure," Jessica said. "Look at the way Simone the Stick is drooling over him. It's positively sickening."

Shelly rolled her eyes. "She probably thinks he's your boyfriend," she remarked, packing up her tote bag. "That would put him on her radar screen for sure."

"I didn't know witches' brooms came equipped with radar."

"You know Simone—always on the cutting edge," Shelly said.

"I'd like to sharpen it for her," Jessica muttered.

"I hate to abandon you here, Jess, but I was supposed to be off ten minutes ago," Shelly said. "I've got to catch my bus. I'll see you tomorrow!"

Shelly strolled out of the studio, swinging her bag. As the door shut behind her Jessica realized she was fresh out of allies. Todd had obviously gone over to the enemy camp. He stood in the sand with Simone, grinning stupidly at her skinny, sulky face. Life wasn't fair. Todd wasn't interested in modeling. He'd always told her it was a dumb ambition. But now there he was, posing in front of the camera. And Jessica wasn't.

Jessica dropped her broom with a clatter, hoping it would break Quentin's concentration. Or Simone's. Or Todd's. But nobody even flinched. She ticked off everything she was miserable about. She despised Simone. She hated the way Simone looked in the five-hundred-dollar Bartucci bikini. She was sick of doing everybody's dirty work. Todd was stealing her modeling career. Her entire body itched from the tiny particles of sand that had worked their way into every article of clothing she wore. Her hair was a mess. And she was furious with Quentin for making Todd a model while he ignored her own much more obvious charms.

Suddenly the door opened. For the first time in hours Jessica perked up. Elizabeth took a few purposeful steps into the room and then froze, her eyes widening at the sight of Simone locking Todd in a tight embrace in front of the garish beach-scene backdrop.

If I have to be miserable, then it's only fair that somebody else should be miserable too, Jessica told herself. Besides, Elizabeth's reaction to Simone and Todd's modeling session would at the very least add some excitement to a long, tedious day.

"And if we're really lucky," Jessica whispered, balling both hands into fists, "Liz will do us all a favor and punch Simone right in her perfect little nose job!"

Elizabeth blinked, fully expecting the hallucination to dissipate like fog. It didn't. Todd was standing in a sandbox, caught in the tight embrace of a tall, gorgeous, and impossibly slim young woman. A woman wearing nothing but a skimpy macramé bikini. Suddenly Elizabeth knew exactly who the siren was. It was Simone, the *Flair* cover girl to whom Jessica had taken such an instant and intense dislike. *The Fashion Witch,* Jessica had called her. For once Elizabeth agreed completely with her sister's assessment.

Elizabeth realized her own mouth was hanging open. She snapped it shut, grateful that nobody except Jessica—a bedraggled, furious-looking Jessica—had even noticed she was in the room. Elizabeth marched up to the set, strengthened by the approval she saw in her sister's eyes.

"Get your hands off my boyfriend!" she demanded.

Todd blushed bright red and jumped off the set as if the sand had caught fire. "L-Liz!" he stammered. "We were just, uh, passing the time waiting for you. Quentin, um, asked me to be a stand-in for his lighting check."

Simone didn't even have the grace to look guilty. "It's been a lot of fun, Todd," she cooed, thrusting one hip forward. "I hope we'll do it again sometime soon."

Todd kept his eyes on Elizabeth's face. "Are you ready to go?" he asked, steering her back toward the door before Simone had a chance to say anything else.

"Todd, don't run out of here so quickly," Quentin called. "I meant what I said about using you as a model. I have a feeling you're going to turn out to be incredibly photogenic."

"Oh, yes, Todd!" Simone echoed. "I just know you are."

"I'll give you a call after I've had a chance to print the shots we took today," Quentin promised Todd. He totally ignored Elizabeth. "If they show what I think they will, I believe you have a promising career ahead of you as a model."

Elizabeth noticed that Jessica's face was turning positively purple.

"We have to go now," Elizabeth said, pulling Todd toward the door. She stopped and fumbled in

108

her purse for a moment. She fished out her car keys and tossed them to Jessica. "I'm riding with Todd. You take the Jeep."

"Can you *believe* it, Liz?" Todd asked as soon as the elevator doors shut behind them. "That photographer, Quentin, really thinks I've got talent as a model. I mean, I can't believe I'm saying this. I never thought models had any talent. But it's a lot harder than it looks, and he says I'm a natural!"

"Um, Todd, if I were you, I wouldn't get my hopes up," Elizabeth said carefully. "Modeling is a very competitive field; most people who are successful at it started out as kids. I wouldn't want you to be disappointed."

"Don't worry about me," Todd replied. "I'm not thinking too much about the future. All I want is to do this now and have some fun—and maybe get out of my boring internship. If something else develops out of these two weeks—well, I'll take it as it comes."

But Elizabeth was worried. And she knew exactly what was developing. She'd seen the way Todd was gazing at Simone—like an adoring puppy. And she'd noticed the way Simone was eyeing Todd—like a bird of prey. Of course Quentin would decide to make Todd a model. In Elizabeth's opinion, Todd was the best-looking guy around. Once he and Simone were working together every day, it was inevitable that he'd fall under the Fashion

Witch's spell. Especially if all Simone's work clothes were as revealing as the macramé bikini.

As they walked to Todd's car he chatted excitedly about the possibility of modeling for Quentin—studiously avoiding any mention of Simone, Elizabeth noticed. She had never seen Todd look so happy and so alive. And she had never felt so rotten.

Chapter 8

Jessica raised her face to the breeze and let the wind toss back her hair. She breathed in the salt air appreciatively. *The real Pacific Ocean makes a much better photo background than Quentin's garishly painted one,* she decided.

"So when do we get started?" Lila asked. "We don't have all night. The sun will set in another hour, and I can't take decent pictures after dark without high-speed film—even if this is the world's most expensive camera."

"I just need a minute to feel clean again," Jessica insisted, reveling in the knowledge that the only sand-covered part of her was the soles of her feet. "You would never believe how disgustingly sweaty and sandy I was this afternoon from creating dunes in Quentin's sandbox."

"And that was supposed to be *work?*" Lila

asked. "Fowler Enterprises doesn't even have a sandbox for its employees. How unenlightened. I should file a complaint with the Labor Department."

"Ha, ha," Jessica said, smoothing down the floral miniskirt that wrapped over the briefs of her pink-and-lavender halter-top bikini. It wasn't a five-hundred-dollar Bartucci bathing suit, but she knew she looked terrific in it.

"What do you do at work *tomorrow?*" Lila asked. "Build sand castles?"

"I don't know about castles, but tomorrow is the day for convincing Prince Charming to ask me out on a date," Jessica planned aloud.

"Charming?" Lila scoffed. "Are you kidding? This Quentin character sounds like an obnoxious control freak."

"OK, so he's not charming," Jessica conceded, checking her face in her mirrored compact. "But he's great looking, and he's totally necessary if I'm going to become a model within the next ten days."

"That's what I like about you, Jess," Lila said. "You don't expect instant gratification of your every wish. You're willing to work for the long-term—"

"Shut up and take pictures," Jessica ordered with a laugh.

"Move a little farther up the beach," Lila instructed. "Your face will be in shadow if the sun is right behind you. That's better. Hold it there. . . . Good. . . . You know, Jess, you are so lucky to have a best friend who's used a superexpensive camera before. You'd be totally stuck if you were expecting anyone else to figure this thing out."

"It would have been easier if you could have brought me your father's camera," Jessica pointed out, throwing one arm behind her head dramatically. "I hated having to borrow this one from Quentin."

"My father took his camera with him on his business trip to Washington, D.C.," Lila said. "But I'm surprised Quentin let you take this one. This thing is worth hundreds of dollars."

Jessica shrugged. She practiced her Simone pout for the camera, stepped forward with one foot, and placed her hands on her hips. "He didn't exactly let me take it," she admitted. "I sort of gave myself permission."

"*What?*" Lila shrieked. "Are you out of what's left of your puny little mind? I'm taking pictures with a stolen camera?"

"*Borrowed*," Jessica corrected. "A *borrowed* camera. Hold on a minute; let me pull off this wrap skirt so you can get my bikini in all its skimpy glory. You should have seen this piece of string Silicone Simone was calling a bathing suit this afternoon. It made her look even more like a toothpick than usual."

"Don't change the subject!" Lila protested. "We were talking about a *felony*. And now I'm an accessory!"

"Speaking of accessories, let me have your rhinestone sunglasses," Jessica said. She slid them on and then pushed the lenses up onto her forehead. "How do I look?"

"Like a felon with good taste," Lila said. "Maybe I should take your mug shot as long as I'm at it. Save the FBI some work."

"Chill out, Li," Jessica urged. "I'll return the camera first thing in the morning, and Quentin will never know the difference. He's got about a million cameras lying around the studios. I bet he can't even tell one from the other. Now let's move into the water so you can take some of me with the waves crashing against my knees."

"Not yet. I'm going to have to put in a new roll of film in a couple of minutes," Lila said. "But are you sure you want me to take this hot camera into the water? Remember, if anything goes wrong with your stolen property, I wasn't here. I never saw this camera. It's totally your responsibility."

"What could go wrong?" Jessica assured her. "Borrowing this camera is the most brilliant idea I ever had!"

"A few days ago the most brilliant idea you ever had was putting together that first scrapbook of photos of yourself. Obviously one monument to your monumental vanity wasn't enough."

Jessica shrugged. "Now it's three days later, and I'm three days more brilliant," she explained.

"You'd better give me back my sunglasses,"

Lila mocked. "Your brilliance is blinding me."

"Now that I'm in the real world of fashion photography, I know that my little scrapbook was too amateurish," Jessica said. "No professional photographer can take you seriously as a supermodel when you're posing in a cheerleading uniform. And the photos could have been taken by my brother. The ones you're doing now will be part of my professional portfolio."

"Do you really think it will make a difference?" Lila asked.

"With these photos I'll knock Simone out of the spotlight in no time," Jessica boasted. "And I hope she lands flat on her smug little face. Come on, let's go in the water now! Do you think I should put my hair up?"

"Ooh, good idea. But leave a few tendrils hanging down in front," Lila advised. "Just give me a minute to load new film." She crouched beside Jessica's backpack and fished out a roll. "You know, it doesn't sound as if Todd needed a professional portfolio to get into the real world of fashion photography," she pointed out as she popped open the back of the camera. "From what you said, Quentin took one look, and he was in the picture."

"Can you *believe* it?" Jessica fumed. Bile rose in her throat every time she thought of Todd, hamming it up with Simone in front of the camera. "How can he see Todd, of all people, as a potential cover boy?"

"I hate to break it to you, Jessica, but your sister's boyfriend is a hunk. And he's got money too. If he had any taste in women, he'd be the perfect guy."

"Todd's OK if *boring* turns you on," Jessica said as they walked into the rolling waves. "But he doesn't have that *jello-say-kwah*."

"I think you mean *je ne sais quoi*," Lila corrected. "It means roughly, 'that certain something.'"

"Well, sorry, Ms. French Scholar. But Todd is a certain *nothing!* He doesn't have that extra spark of personality that I have. He has *zero* charisma!"

Lila rolled her eyes. "If anyone should be a fashion model, it's me," she said. "I have more experience trying on expensive clothes than anyone."

Jessica remembered a time when a modeling agency representative had told Lila she wasn't photogenic enough to be a model. But she forced herself not to bring it up. Being turned down as a cover girl for *Ingenue* magazine was a sore spot with Lila. And Jessica needed Lila's help now, not her wrath. She put her arm around her friend's shoulders. "I promise that as soon as I'm famous, I'll bring you along for the ride."

"Gee, *thanks*," Lila said cynically. "As long as we're getting soaked you might as well do some more posing. Why don't you splash around a little?"

"OK, but keep your distance," Jessica said. "We can't afford to get that camera wet."

"The camera? I was more worried about my hair," Lila replied. "These waves are getting higher. I'm glad I wore shorts."

"Just keep that thing on the strap around your neck," Jessica cautioned as she splashed water on her upper body. "Take some of me wet, like those bathing-suit models in the sports magazines. Here, get this!" She allowed a wave to gently lift her off the ocean floor as she tilted her face into the setting sun.

"You just jump and splash around. Keep your face dry, and let me worry about when to click the shutter," Lila instructed. "I know what I'm doing."

"Ooh! Look at that big wave coming our way!" Jessica called. "I'm going to bodysurf this one. Make sure you get a good angle. The left side of my face is my best side."

"Big wave?" Lila cried, turning in horror to see it bearing down on her. "*Jessica!*" She ran for the shore—too late. The wave crashed over her, tumbling Lila's slender body over and over in the sand. A moment later she was sitting in a few inches of water with a dazed expression on her face, her long, light brown hair plastered to her shoulders. Water streamed from her hair, her face, and her silk T-shirt. And it streamed from the camera that still hung around her neck.

117

"Oh, no!" Jessica screamed. "Lila, is the camera all right?"

"I'm touched by your concern," Lila spluttered. "I could have been *drowned*. And my hair is *ruined!*"

Jessica unlooped the camera from around her friend's neck. "It's full of water! Do you think it will dry?"

"Face it, Jess," Lila seethed. "It's ruined. You should have stolen a waterproof camera."

"This can't be happening!" Jessica wailed, inspecting the camera from every angle. "Lila, lend me the money to buy Quentin a new one!"

"Obviously your brain is waterlogged," Lila told her. "I will *not* lend you the money. You already owe me for this silk top. I thought you were taking complete responsibility for your actions this time?"

Jessica closed her eyes and dropped to her knees, clutching the soggy camera. "I'm *toast*," she said glumly.

"The set designer, Kevin, is teaching me all about how to paint scenery so that it looks real," Maria told Elizabeth that evening as they sat on the edge of the pool at the Wakefields' house. She was only two days into her internship at the Bridgewater Theatre Group, but she had already learned more about backstage work than she'd thought possible. "The set we're working on is made of plywood and Styrofoam," she said. "But it looks exactly like marble!"

"I saw the set in the photography studio today," Elizabeth said. Her eyes were fixed on the sparkling water of the pool, but the expression in them was far away. "Quentin set up kind of a stylized beach—not that anyone would notice the scenery, with that tiny scrap of a bikini Simone was wearing."

"Get your mind off it," Maria urged, kicking at the water with her foot. "Concentrate on how much you're learning in your own department. You know, until this internship I never knew how much I could enjoy this side of theatrical work. Actors are so caught up in what they're doing that they don't realize how much work goes into the rest of the production."

"Todd tried to tell me how much work it is to model," Elizabeth said. "As if he was some sort of expert after being a stand-in at a lighting check for an hour."

Maria sighed. "Let me tell you more about Kevin," she said. "I'm learning so much from him. He—"

"I'm learning a lot from Leona too," Elizabeth interrupted. "I really admire her. I've never met a woman who's so sure of herself. She knows exactly where she wants to go. And she'll do whatever it takes to get there."

"Sounds a little too single-minded to me," Maria cautioned. "I met a lot of people like that in

Hollywood. They act like your best friend as long as they think you can help them. But as soon as you turn around, they'll stab you in the back."

Elizabeth turned on her with an intensity that made Maria sit up straight. "You don't even *know* her!" she cried. "Leona's not like that. She genuinely wants to help young women just entering the field. She wants to help *me!*"

"Sorry," Maria said, surprised. "I didn't mean to diss Leona specifically. Some people really do want to help. Kevin, for example. He knows everything there is to know about backstage work. And I don't think I mentioned that he is unbelievably cute—"

"Cute isn't everything," Elizabeth said, interrupting her again. "Todd is cute. But today he was a real jerk. That bimbo had her hands all over him. Not only did he let her do it, but he *liked* it!"

"Have you heard even a single word I've said?" Maria asked, annoyed. "We've talked about nothing but *Flair* magazine for the last two days! Every time I try to tell you what I'm doing, you change the subject back."

"I'm sorry," Elizabeth apologized. "I guess I'm preoccupied. You were telling me about the set painter?"

"He's the set *designer,*" Maria corrected. "Kevin's a university student, working at the theater for college credit. And I've been saving the best for last—he asked me out!" She smiled the dazzling smile that had sold millions of rolls of Softee toilet paper. But Elizabeth didn't notice; she was intent on picking at the hem of her shorts. "It's only lunch," Maria continued, glaring pointedly at her friend. "But you've got to start somewhere."

"Quentin is supposed to know what he's talking about," Elizabeth said glumly. "And he says Todd has a future as a model. I just can't see it."

"Why not?" Maria asked, losing patience. She jumped up from the edge of the pool and sat in a folding chair nearby, crossing her arms in front of her. "That man of yours is just as good-looking as any of the actors I worked with in films. If he wants to try modeling, why shouldn't he?"

"But he's not a model!" Elizabeth argued. "He's just a normal guy. He always said models were brainless and conceited."

"So, he changed his mind."

"What if he changes his mind about me too?"

Maria rolled her eyes. "Liz, you're not making any sense. Todd loves you. So what if he likes it when a supermodel runs her hands all over him? What guy wouldn't? It's not like anything happened. They were in a roomful of people!"

"You're right," Elizabeth agreed quietly. "Nothing happened. But what if it does?"

"What if we have an earthquake tomorrow and

the whole state slides into the Pacific Ocean?" Maria countered. "You can't deal in what-ifs!"

Elizabeth sighed. "I know."

"Personally, I'm not thinking any further ahead than my lunch with Kevin tomorrow. We're going to an artsy little bistro a block down from the theater." Maria clenched her jaw when she noticed that Elizabeth's eyes had a faraway look again. "After a lunch of snake gizzards and poison toadstools," she continued, "I thought we'd hijack the space shuttle and fly to Jupiter for dessert."

"That's nice," Elizabeth murmured. "The scary thing is that deep down, I'm afraid Todd is seriously attracted to Simone. She's drop-dead gorgeous, and she's famous—"

"That's it!" Maria yelled, jumping to her feet. "I am so *fed up* with your attitude. You know, Liz," she scolded, shaking her finger, "if you weren't so caught up in yourself lately, maybe Todd wouldn't be enjoying another girl's attention so much!"

"What do you know about it?" Elizabeth screamed back, tears of frustration in her eyes. "You don't understand the pressures of the *real* world. Interning at a rinky-dink community theater isn't like working somewhere *important*, like *Flair*!"

Maria slitted her eyes. "Important?" she asked in a low, controlled voice. "You've lost all sense of what's *really* important." She spun on her heel and stomped away.

"Quentin is crazy if he thinks he can make Todd into a model," Elizabeth muttered on Wednesday morning as she merged the Jeep into a rush-hour traffic jam on the Santa Monica Freeway. "Todd doesn't know the first thing about modeling."

"I'll say!" Jessica agreed. "He looked like a total dweeb, posing with Silicone Simone yesterday. How am I ever going to get Quentin to notice me if he's too busy trying to put Todd's boring face all over the newsstands?"

"Boring?" Elizabeth protested, a twinge of loyalty rising in her chest. "This *is* my boyfriend we're talking about."

Jessica rolled her eyes. "So? You said you're mad at him. I thought we were in agreement here."

"We are, I guess." Elizabeth relented. "But we're the only ones who are. Even before he lost his mind over Simone and this modeling idea, Todd was a pain in the neck. He doesn't understand the kind of pressure I'm under, trying to make a good impression on Leona."

"Lila is clueless about working in the real world too," Jessica complained. She leaned over to honk the horn at a slow truck driver in front of the Jeep, but Elizabeth pushed her hand away. "Lila doesn't see why it's so important for me to get on Quentin's good side," Jessica concluded.

"Maria came over yesterday afternoon, and she was no help at all," Elizabeth added. "You're the only person around who has any idea what it's like in the real world."

"Enid's at a real literary agency," Jessica said. "It's part of the real publishing world—even if it is a boring part. Didn't she call last night for one of those long, dull gab sessions that put me to sleep when I listen in on the extension?"

"Jessica!" Elizabeth protested.

"I didn't listen last night!" Jessica assured her.

"There was nothing to listen to," Elizabeth said with a sigh. "I thought Enid might understand what we're up against at *Flair.*"

"Does she?" Jessica asked.

"She called to tell me about some dumb manuscript, but she knows nothing about deadline pressure," Elizabeth replied. "I could tell she was ticked off when I said I couldn't talk. Maybe I was rude to her, but I had *Flair*'s 'Fashion Flops' section to proofread. I didn't have time for trivial conversations."

"Lila knows nothing about *any* kind of pressure," Jessica said. "She really ought to help me make things right with Quentin. It's not like she can't afford it."

"Make what things right with Quentin?" Elizabeth asked, steering the Jeep into an open spot in the next lane.

"I sort of borrowed a camera from him," Jessica

explained. "And Lila sort of dropped it in the ocean."

Elizabeth's eyes grew larger. "You ruined his camera?"

"Sort of," Jessica admitted. "Look, Liz. My entire career hangs in the balance here. I have to replace Quentin's camera, or he'll never give me my big break!"

"If you don't replace it fast, he may break some bones," Elizabeth pointed out.

"Lend me the money," Jessica pleaded. "You've got a ton saved up for that new computer."

"Not anymore," Elizabeth said, gesturing toward her stylishly long blazer and short skirt.

"Rats." Jessica sighed. "I'm doomed."

"Lila's got more money than the Federal Reserve," Elizabeth reminded her. "And you said she was the one who wrecked the camera. Can't you get it from her?"

"Lila doesn't understand the seriousness of the situation," Jessica said huffily. "And she claims the camera was my responsibility. Some loyal friend!"

"I know what you mean," Elizabeth replied, nodding. "These internships are teaching me a lot about friendship and loyalty that I was in no hurry to learn."

"Me too," Jessica agreed. "It's been an eye-opening experience, that's for sure."

Chapter 9

Jessica knew she was in trouble before she even reached the photography studio Wednesday morning. From the hallway she could hear Quentin's voice. Long before she could make out his words, she could tell he was haranguing an employee.

She slipped inside the studio, willing herself to be invisible. Quentin's back was to her as he yelled at an assistant. "Photographic equipment doesn't walk away on its own!" he shouted at a cowering man nearly twice his age. "Somebody misplaced that camera or walked out of here with it. And I intend to find out who!"

Jessica cringed. She'd hoped it would take him a few days to realize that the camera was missing. She didn't even know how he could tell them all apart. Now other employees were skirting around the edges of the room, trying to do their jobs while keeping out of Quentin's path. Jessica decided that was an excellent idea. Certainly this would not be a good time to try to seduce Quentin into asking her out.

Simone was the only person in the room who didn't seem concerned about Quentin's tirade. She was languishing on the couch, chomping on her celery and sipping from a bottle of mineral water. Her expression held nothing but pure boredom; she didn't seem the least bit interested in Quentin's problem. *No doubt,* Jessica figured, *she knows she's above suspicion.*

"Has anyone seen those proofs of me in Lina Lapin's latest?" Simone drawled. "They should be up from the mail room by now."

Her expression darkened when nobody responded. Jessica could see that Simone hated it when anybody else was the center of attention. Jessica rolled her eyes. Surely even a supermodel could lift a telephone receiver to call the mail room without overburdening her skinny little body too much. *Maybe it's too complicated a task for her skinny little brain,* Jessica thought.

Quentin's eye fell on Shelly. The unhappy photography assistant who'd been bearing the brunt of his anger scampered away. "Shelly!" the head photographer shouted, storming across the room. The African American girl stood in her usual corner, setting up her makeup table. "Have you touched my Minolta? The big one, with the telephoto?"

"Sorry, Quentin," said the makeup assistant in a low voice, keeping her eyes on her jars and tubes. "I haven't seen it. I don't touch anything that doesn't remove with cold cream."

Quentin hardly listened to her answer but launched into an angry explanation of where he'd last seen the camera and demanding to know if Shelly had noticed anyone in that room.

Jessica was getting nervous. Sooner or later— probably sooner—Quentin would pounce on her. And even her well-practiced skill at concealing the truth might falter under his furious gaze.

"Isn't anybody going to see what's keeping the mail room from delivering those proofs?" Simone called out again in a louder voice.

Jessica jumped. She hated complying with one of Simone's prima donna requests. But it would be a good way to remove herself from Quentin's reach. *And I wouldn't mind seeing Cameron again,* she mused. *But only because he was fun to talk to. As a friend,* she reminded herself. She wasn't the least bit interested in any mail-room clerk as anything more than a friend.

"I'll go down there right now, Simone," she offered, keeping her voice low so as not to attract Quentin's attention.

"It's about time you started paying attention when I give an order," Simone said smugly. "Interns are supposed to be here so that the important people don't have to waste our time on trivia."

129

"Of course," Jessica said sweetly. "We wouldn't want to tax you with any real work." She slipped back toward the door before Simone could reply, taking care to keep out of Quentin's line of sight. On her way out she grabbed a photography catalog from a rack in the corner. She needed to know exactly how much the ruined camera was worth in case she found a way to get her hands on the money.

Jessica pressed every button in the elevator to drag out the trip for as long as possible. If Quentin was already busy with his morning meeting before she returned, then he wouldn't be able to question her about the camera until later. Besides, she could use the time to find the right camera in the catalog. If Simone questioned her about her lateness in returning, she could always exclaim truthfully, "I'm so sorry! I swear that elevator stopped on every single floor on the way down."

Once on the first floor Jessica walked as slowly as she could to the mail area. Then she scouted the cluttered main room, peering through doorways into some of the adjoining rooms. She didn't see Cameron anywhere. But she reminded herself sternly that it didn't matter. She wasn't interested in Cameron. He was probably delivering a package somewhere in the building.

"Oh, well," she said under her breath, "I'll just find Simone's proofs myself." From Monday afternoon she remembered where Cameron kept the newly arrived overnight packages. She searched through the pile until she came to a thick envelope marked Photographs, addressed to Quentin's department. She imagined dozens of copies of Simone's surgically enhanced pout inside and shuddered. But at least Simone's face was giving her a reason to stay away from the photo studio. Now all she needed was an excuse to stay away awhile longer—until she could be sure that Quentin was in his meeting.

Out of the corner of her eye she spotted a telephone behind the main counter. If she couldn't talk to a cute mail-room worker, she could at least call Lila and beg her, one last time, to lend her the money to replace Quentin's waterlogged camera.

Cameron hunched in front of a computer screen, tracking an overnight package that should have arrived at *Flair* first thing Wednesday morning and had not. The software was new, and it took all his concentration to figure out which keys to push. Out in the main part of the mail room somebody was shuffling around. Cameron gave a silent thanks for his secluded computer alcove, tucked behind some shelves and nearly invisible from most of the main room. If he stopped his search now, he would have to start all over again. Whoever was in the mail room could wait.

After a few minutes he had what he needed. The first two digits in the zip code had been transposed; the package had gone to Delaware instead of California. He punched in a few more commands to have the box rerouted. Then he stood up, stretched, and stepped around the cluttered shelves to see whoever was waiting for him.

A woman stood near the counter, cradling the telephone against her shoulder. Her back was turned to him, but Cameron knew of only one person with such beautiful golden hair.

"Lila, it's me," Jessica said into the receiver.

"*Yes*, I'm going to ask you about the camera again," she said after a pause.

"But you're my *best friend!*" she wailed. "Besides, *you* were the one who dropped Quentin's camera and ruined it."

"I know it wasn't *exactly* your fault—," Jessica began, but her friend obviously interrupted her. She twirled a lock of hair around one finger while she waited.

"OK, OK, it wasn't your fault at all," Jessica admitted finally. "I *know!* I'm the one who borrowed it without asking. How many times do you have to remind me of that?"

"Come on, Lila! I swear I'll pay you back, even if it takes the rest of my life!" she promised. "But it won't take that long. I'll have plenty of money soon."

"What do you mean, *how*?" Jessica responded a

moment later. "We must've gotten at least one good roll of photos last night, right? With you taking the pictures, I'm sure they'll be awesome. They'll be delivered here tomorrow, and then I'll put together a professional portfolio. I'll be rolling in modeling contracts in no time!".

"Yes," she said with a loud sigh, answering a query from her friend. "I know about my rotten credit history. *Everyone* knows about my rotten credit history! But credit histories shouldn't matter between friends! Especially when it's such a teensy-weensy amount of money—to *you* anyway. You know you could afford to buy every one of Quentin's cameras and *still* have cash left over for film!"

As Lila replied, Jessica pulled a dog-eared booklet from her pocket.

"Yes, as a matter of fact I *do* know what it costs," Jessica replied, opening the booklet to a page with a turned-down corner. "I've got a sales catalog right here, with the exact model and price of the Minolta you—*we* ruined."

She paused, and Cameron knew from the slump of her shoulders that she didn't like her friend's response.

"Aw, Lila!" Jessica said, her voice rising. "When Quentin finds out it was me, he'll strangle me with a camera strap. And probably fire me. But if I can replace that camera today, he won't have to know."

"Yeah, *right*. Thanks a bunch." She dropped the

receiver back onto its hook and rested her head forlornly on her arms. "What am I supposed to do now?" she wailed. She looked so sad that Cameron wanted to run over and hold her. Before he could move, she straightened up and gave a loud, long sigh. Then she ripped the catalog in two and tossed it in the trash can.

Cameron ducked back behind the shelves and watched thoughtfully as Jessica trudged out of the room. She walked as if she were heading to a firing squad.

At noon that day Elizabeth studied the newsstand of a drugstore a block away from the Mode building. She had already read as many issues of *Flair* as she could get her hands on at the office. *Now,* she decided, *it's time to see what the competition's doing.* Maybe she could find out what worked well for other magazines and build on those ideas to help Leona make *Flair* even better. If she could come up with just one great suggestion, she was sure Leona would seriously consider hiring her for a summer job.

She reached for a copy of *Dazzle* and thumbed through it. The "Letters to the Editor" section was longer than Flair's, with more readers' responses to articles they'd seen in the magazine. But the photography throughout the magazine was weak, and the articles weren't as well written as the ones in *Flair*. Elizabeth could see why *Flair* had outpaced *Dazzle*'s sales so quickly.

Fashion Forward, she saw, was advertising its own interactive Web page. Readers could call it up on their computers, see footage from the most recent fashion shows, and vote on the clothes they liked best. *Flair* was already available on the Internet, but there was no forum for readers to register their own views.

Next she paged through a copy of *Bella,* one of the hottest-selling magazines in the business. She stopped at a page titled "Woman on the Street." Each month a reporter chose one question to ask a variety of ordinary women from all walks of life. This month, Elizabeth saw, the question was about hemlines and just how high they should be.

"Now that's not a bad idea," she said in a low voice. Then she looked up, embarrassed that she'd spoken out loud. A salesclerk glared at her from the counter. He wasn't near enough to have heard her words, but he was watching her with narrow eyes and obviously had been for some time.

"Pick a magazine and buy it!" the sour-faced man instructed. "I'm not running a lending library here."

Elizabeth smiled and nodded. "Sorry," she said. "I've almost decided."

In Elizabeth's opinion the length of a skirt wasn't a scintillating topic of discussion. And a one-line response wasn't enough space for exploring an issue and expressing a viewpoint. But she liked *Bella*'s concept of asking the opinion of real people—not the usual models and designers whose faces were already all over the pages of the fashion press. How could she adapt that idea to use in *Flair*?

Suddenly Elizabeth remembered a discussion Mr. Collins had led with some of the staff of the *Oracle*, Sweet Valley High's student newspaper. Mr. Collins, her favorite teacher and the newspaper adviser, had told them about community journalism, a new trend in newspapers that got readers involved with their local newspaper and pushed the newspaper into a higher level of involvement with the community. Elizabeth hadn't been sure how she felt about a newspaper being involved in community events rather than remaining an objective observer. But she'd liked the part about getting more readers' viewpoints into the newspaper.

Now she realized that all the elements that had impressed her in the competing fashion magazines did just that. They gave the readers a forum for sharing opinions and hearing what other people—regular people, not experts or celebrities—were thinking. And an idea began to take shape in her mind.

"Could I get you a cappuccino and an easy chair so you can be comfortable while you read that?" asked the sarcastic salesclerk.

"Uh, sorry," Elizabeth apologized weakly, holding out the copy of *Bella*. "I'll take this one."

❖   ❖   ❖

Todd stood at a bank of file cabinets in the executive suite of Varitronics. He opened a folder of expense reports from a recent trip several of the vice presidents had made to Singapore. "One copy to accounting; one to each VP's file," he chanted aloud, repeating the instructions he'd received from Meeks.

The first expense report was from Harriet Roy, the firm's vice president of manufacturing. "*R*," he said aloud, scanning the file cabinets for the correct drawer. "Where are the *Rs*?"

This is ridiculous, Todd reflected. How could any adult with half a brain put up with such a boring job? Even as a junior in high school he was overqualified for alphabetizing files. *Any seven-year-old could do this job,* he told himself. *A trained chimpanzee could do this job. Even Jessica and Lila could do this job!*

"I have to get out of here!" he said under his breath. Suddenly he understood what was behind the reports he'd heard about mild-mannered office workers in various parts of the country suffering breakdowns and showing up at work with machine guns. "Todd was such a quiet boy," he could imagine his friends and neighbors telling reporters. "He always seemed so normal."

If he didn't find a way to cut short this internship soon, they would have to drag him away from Varitronics in a straitjacket.

A phone rang—or rather *beeped*. Even the

telephones in this office were abnormal. From across the room he recognized the sound as the phone in his own cubicle. He dropped the file and sprinted toward the cubicle, remembering Meeks's rule that phones had to be answered in two rings. On the way there he stubbed his toe against the thin wall of a neighboring cubicle and stumbled, nearly hurling himself to the carpet. He caught himself just in time. As he hopped into his cubicle on his unhurt foot he grabbed the phone as it rang a third time. So much for Meeks's rules. Then he fell into the creaky office chair, holding his foot in one hand and the telephone receiver in another.

He ignored a giggle coming from the woman in the next cubicle.

"Hello!" he barked into the phone. "Um, I mean, Varitronics. May I help you?"

"This is Quentin Berg, calling for Mr. Todd Wilkins," said the voice of the photographer he'd met the day before.

"Yes, Mr. Berg!" Todd said, suddenly psyched. He forgot about the pain in his toe. "What can I do for you?"

"For starters, call me Quentin," answered the photographer. "After that, well, it looks like I've got a modeling job for you if you're interested."

Todd took a deep breath. He'd sweep sand into dunes for Quentin if it would get him out of Varitronics. As for posing with a gorgeous young woman in a bikini while a roomful of people told him how handsome he was—well, he thought he could handle that. "Yes, sir!" he replied eagerly. "I'm very interested."

"Good," Quentin said. "But the shoot's this afternoon. I'll need you at my studio right away so we can get your hair and makeup done. Can you make it?"

"I'm leaving now!" Todd answered with a grin.

He was already pulling off his tie when he called his father's voice mail a minute later.

"Sorry to break this to you, Dad," he said in response to the recorded message. "But I'm quitting my Varitronics internship. Another job has come up, and I'm sure I can sell the teachers on it back at school. There might be a real future in this. I'll tell you all about it tonight."

Elizabeth took a deep breath and marched up to Leona's door. She'd rushed back to the office from the newsstand and had spent the last half hour mapping out her new idea for *Flair*. Deep down, Elizabeth thought it was a wonderful suggestion. On the other hand, she was only a high-school student. What did she know about running a professional fashion magazine? What if her idea was stupid?

"What if Leona hates it?" she asked under her breath. *Well*, she decided, *there's only one way to find out*. She knocked on the door, and Leona told her to come in.

The managing editor gestured to a chair. "Sit down, Elizabeth," she said. "Would you like a cup of coffee?"

"No, thanks," Elizabeth said. She was jittery enough already. "I'm sorry to bother you. I can come back later if this isn't a good time—"

Leona smiled reassuringly. "Of course this is a good time. What can I do for you?"

"I . . . um . . . had an idea for the magazine," Elizabeth stammered. "And I wanted to run it by you."

"That's wonderful, Elizabeth," Leona said. "I meant it when I said I welcome suggestions. Tell me what's on your mind."

"I thought it would be great if we allowed one reader each month to write a column in *Flair*," she blurted. As she spoke she warmed to her subject and felt herself growing more confident and articulate. "We already show our audience how the models and clothing designers interpret style. But we don't have any way for women to see how other people—people just like them—view fashion. Each month a different reader would write about fashion and how it affects her life."

Leona had a thoughtful look on her face. "Do you have a name for this column?" she asked.

"My working title is 'Free Style,'" Elizabeth replied. "But of course, you could call it anything you want."

"Why do you think our readers and advertisers

would like to see something like this ·in *Flair?*"
Leona probed.

"We're not as interactive as many other publications," Elizabeth explained. "This monthly column would be a forum for making readers feel more involved in the magazine. Yesterday I read in *Publishing Age* that readers are more likely to continue buying the magazine if they feel that they're a part of it. And that will help us hold on to advertisers."

"Have you thought about the costs of starting up a new column?" Leona asked. She sounded like Mr. Collins in English class, making sure his students had thought through their views. And like Mr. Collins, her voice was so nonjudgmental that Elizabeth couldn't tell if the editor liked her idea.

"The art director would have to come up with a design—a new look for 'Free Style,'" Elizabeth said. "But it would fit the same general format as the other columns, so the design wouldn't be a major outlay of time."

"And the manuscripts themselves?" Leona asked in that same tone of noncommittal questioning.

"I've been looking into what other magazines pay, and I believe we can get good-quality writing for much less than what professional fashion writers normally charge," Elizabeth said quickly. She held out the notes in her hand. "I've recommended some amounts if you'd like to see—"

"Later," Leona said with an encouraging smile. "Right now tell me more about the general idea. How would we ensure the quality of the writing?"

"Of course, the writers wouldn't be professionals," Elizabeth said. "The manuscripts might require a little more editing than usual. But if we restrict the column to one page in the magazine, that wouldn't take a lot of time."

"At least you've done your homework," Leona said diplomatically. "I'm proud of the way you anticipated my questions and had answers ready."

"But?" Elizabeth asked, sensing that the editor wasn't saying everything that was on her mind.

Leona took a deep breath. "I don't want to discourage your creativity, Elizabeth," she began. "But it's not really up to me. I'll run your idea by the editor in chief. But my instincts tell me that it isn't going to fly. The editor feels very strongly about maintaining the high quality of writing in *Flair*. It's one of the things that distinguishes us from our competitors."

Elizabeth felt as if she'd been kicked in the stomach. "Oh," she said in a small voice. Leona was too polite to say it was a rotten idea, but Elizabeth got the message. She concentrated very hard on not crying.

"May I have the notes on the research you've done?" Leona asked. "They might help when I meet with the editor. But don't get your hopes up, Elizabeth. And please feel free to come back with any other suggestions that occur to you."

Elizabeth trudged back to her office, staring at the floor. Leona had been as kind and encouraging as always. But she'd made it clear that Elizabeth's idea would never find its way into the pages of *Flair.* Elizabeth sank into her desk chair. "My first idea is a failure," she whispered, still fighting tears. A half hour earlier she'd been so excited about "Free Style." Now she felt utterly defeated. For the first time she seriously wondered if she had any real talent.

Her eyes fell on Todd's fax, still taped to the wall over her computer. "You've got too much talent to waste," he'd written, as if in answer to her unspoken question. "I hope your internship is everything you want it to be."

She wiped the tears from her eyes and resolved to keep trying. She still had seven days left in her internship. She would just have to try harder to come up with an idea that was truly exceptional.

In the meantime she was glad that she and Todd had a date planned for that night. The fax reminded her of how much she loved him. She knew she needed to get away from the office and relax a little. Even more than that, she needed to make things up to Todd. *Maria's right,* Elizabeth decided. *I have been too hard on him about the modeling.* And the tension between them now hung over her head like a storm cloud. Tonight was her chance to clear the air. She and Todd would spend a nice evening together and she would apologize for overreacting. He would give her one of his superdeluxe kisses. And then everything would be fine.

Chapter 10

Jessica checked the clock on the wall of the photography studio. It was nearly two o'clock. She'd managed to keep out of Quentin's way so far. Sooner or later he would realize she was the only person on his staff who hadn't been questioned about his missing camera. And when he finally did, she wasn't sure she could keep the truth from showing on her face.

She decided that her best strategy was to keep avoiding him. In the meantime she still hoped she'd come up with a lot of money—or a brilliant plan—before Quentin confronted her. The best way to avoid Quentin, she'd realized in the past two days, was to anticipate his every wish. The only time he seemed to notice her was when he needed her to do something.

Photo shoot this afternoon, she reminded

herself under her breath. *So what needs to be done?* Today's shoot would use the same set as yesterday, she remembered, but with Todd as a real model instead of a stand-in. Quentin had been so impressed with the pictures from Tuesday afternoon that he'd canceled his professional model for today. At the moment Todd was in Michael's salon, having his hair styled.

Suddenly Jessica knew what she could be working on to keep Quentin from having a reason to yell at her. The sandbox from yesterday was still set up. But Jessica's sand dunes seemed to have eroded slightly overnight. She knew the photographer would want them to be perfect. She sighed loudly and headed for the broom in the corner, trying to console herself with thoughts of what a wonderful "how-I-got-my-start" anecdote this would make when she was a supermodel being interviewed on a late-night talk show. They didn't help.

She picked up the broom and trudged to the sandbox to sweep the dunes back into shape.

"You're not planning to fly out of here on that thing, are you?" Simone asked, gesturing toward the broom.

Jessica cursed her luck. She hadn't noticed the model come in. "You made a joke, Simone," she replied. "That's very good. I guess you finally found two brain cells to rub together."

Jessica was sure that for just an instant, she saw

146

a hint of fury in Simone's cold eyes. *Score one for the Wakefield twin!* Jessica thought with glee. With Quentin out of sight, she couldn't think of a single reason to be nice to the Fashion Fink.

"Simone, I've been waiting for you!" Shelly called from the makeup room. "Quentin wants to start shooting in half an hour. You'd better hurry."

Simone's usual mask of disdain fell back over her face. The model didn't reply to either Jessica or Shelly. She cast a cold, superior glance in Jessica's direction. Then she turned and sauntered to the makeup artist, hips leading the way. Jessica realized that she'd just made a serious enemy of Simone. But she really didn't care. Quentin would probably murder her within the next half hour. Or at least fire her. Either way, she wouldn't have to worry about the wrath of the supermodel.

"The Wrath of the Supermodel," she said under her breath, repeating the thought as she stepped gingerly into the sandbox and began brushing sand toward her drooping dunes. "That's a great name for a horror movie." Simone would be the supermodel returned from the dead, sentenced to saunter through eternity, casting cold-eyed pouts on innocent young teens. They would run in terror, screaming into the night—

"Jessica!" called Quentin's voice behind her.

Jessica jumped, her feet sliding in the sand.

"I'm fixing up these sand dunes right now, Quentin," she responded, pretending to be intent on her work. She crossed her fingers on the broom handle, praying that he wouldn't have time before the shoot to ask her about his Minolta. "These dunes will be absolutely perfect before you're ready to begin," she assured him.

From behind her Quentin placed a hand on Jessica's shoulder. She nearly jumped out of the sandbox. There was no telling what he might do to her if he'd discovered she took his missing camera.

"Don't worry about the sand dunes," Quentin said. Jessica froze. His voice sounded almost . . . *nice*. "You did such a terrific job on them yesterday that they still look fine," he continued. She whirled, expecting to see a Quentin clone or another staff member yelling, "April fool!" But the real Quentin Berg was standing there. And around his neck hung the fancy Minolta camera she'd borrowed the night before. The camera she'd ruined. Except that it looked perfect. In fact, it looked new. Her eyes widened.

"Your camera—," she began, pointing to it.

"I wanted to thank you for what you did with it, Jessica," Quentin said, a grin lighting his face as he stroked the camera. Even in her current state of shock Jessica noticed that he was even cuter when he smiled. She couldn't remember seeing him smile before. She'd never noticed his eyes before either. They were a deep, mysterious gray. "I somehow missed you when I asked everyone about the camera this morning," he continued. "If I'd talked to you, I could have saved myself a lot of frustration."

Jessica was beginning to wonder if she'd dreamed the whole incident with Lila at the beach. Now she had a terrible urge to hum the theme song from *The Twilight Zone*.

"But that's all right," Quentin said. "I found the camera on the desk where you left it, and I got your note about how you saw that it needed a thorough cleaning and overhaul." He held up the camera. "You did a terrific job on this! If I didn't know better, I'd swear it was a brand-new camera."

"I . . . uh . . . knew how meticulous you are about your equipment," Jessica said weakly, her mind racing for an explanation. Maybe her fantasy about the undead wasn't far off. But even in zombie form Simone wouldn't lift a finger to solve a problem for Jessica. Maybe the camera was still ruined, and what she was experiencing now was a hallucination.

"I have never had an intern who was astute enough to notice that my equipment needed work and to take the initiative like this," Quentin said, gesturing with the note she had supposedly written him. "If you'd asked me, I would have told you not to touch my cameras. But you really knew what you were doing! This is in perfect working condition."

Suddenly Jessica had visions of being asked to take apart and clean every one of Quentin's cameras. "Actually I didn't do the work myself," she admitted. Suddenly a vague theory began forming in her mind about the source of the new camera. "I . . . uh . . . asked a friend who knows about things like that."

"Well, your friend did a really professional job!" Quentin exclaimed. "And now I see that you've been doing one too. I'm afraid I've been remiss in not taking more interest in your work here."

"Quentin!" Shelly called from a doorway. "Do you want anything special on Simone's eye makeup?"

"Gotta go, Jessica," Quentin said with a wink. Then he turned and practically skipped off to the makeup room.

Jessica stared after him, flabbergasted. After a moment she realized her mouth was hanging open. She snapped it shut, glad that nobody had noticed. Then she saw something on the floor and stooped to pick it up. It was the note she had supposedly left for Quentin when she returned his camera. It was signed with her name, but she'd never seen the note before.

Todd stood in the sand, feeling awkward. He was wearing a pair of black-and-red Bartucci swim trunks that luckily were less revealing than the bathing suit Simone had modeled the day before. At the moment Simone was nowhere in sight. Quentin was loading film into a camera, his assistants were adjusting lights, and Jessica was helping Shelly set out makeup on a table for touch-ups. Todd was the only person in the room with nothing to do. And he was the only one wearing nothing but a bathing suit.

Screens had been set up in two corners for costume changes. Suddenly Simone stepped out from behind hers. And without meaning to, Todd whistled.

Simone's eyes were outlined in something dark and sultry looking. Her full, sensuous lips were the same shade of red as her bathing suit. And her hair swung enchantingly around her bare white shoulders. But Todd was having trouble keeping his eyes on her face. The tall, slender model looked incredible in a bright red one-piece bathing suit that had huge geometric shapes cut out of it, as if someone at the clothing factory had gone crazy with a pair of scissors. He didn't know how practical it would be for swimming. But he sure didn't mind the extra glimpses it allowed of Simone's flawless ivory skin.

The makeup on his own skin felt odd, as if he were wearing a mask over his face. But Shelly had assured him it would look perfectly natural under the bright lights. *And she must be right,* he decided. Since he'd stepped out from behind his own dressing screen, so many people had complimented Todd on his appearance that he realized he must be better looking than he'd thought.

These people worked with professional models every day. If they said he had great hair, a great face, and a great body—well, who was he to argue? Of course, Elizabeth had always said those things. But she was his girlfriend. She had to say nice things about him. He wondered how he'd managed to go all these years without knowing he was a very handsome guy.

"Jessica, there's no bathrobe in there for me to wear between takes!" Simone barked.

Jessica rolled her eyes. "I'll get one from the wardrobe room," she said in a controlled voice. She scurried off.

The model's features and voice smoothed into silk as she sauntered toward Todd. She stepped onto the sand and linked her arm around his. "Hi, good-looking," she greeted him. He'd never been so close to a woman who was nearly as tall as he was. It was strangely exciting to see her eyes so close to his and to feel her breath on his cheek. "Are you ready to play in the sandbox with me?" she purred into his ear. "Later we can see what develops in the darkroom."

Todd gulped. This had to be a dream.

And he was in no hurry to wake up.

❖   ❖   ❖

"Can you believe the way he's acting?" Jessica whispered to Shelly as they watched Todd and Simone cavort in the sand in front of Quentin's camera. "I've never seen him so gaga over any-one—not even my sister!"

"He's not the only one," Shelly whispered back. "I've never seen the Silicone Queen hang all over a male model like that."

"Great chemistry, you two!" Quentin called out to his models as he dropped to one knee to shoot from a lower angle. "Keep it coming!"

"Jessica," Simone called from the set, "you picked out the wrong sunglasses. Run to the wardrobe room and get me another pair! These don't fit; they pinch my ears."

"Sorry about that, Simone," Jessica replied. "I guess your head is even bigger than I thought."

Simone glared.

"Good emotion, Simone!" Quentin called. "It's real. It's intense. Lots of energy!"

"I'd like to give her some good emotions," Jessica whispered to Shelly as she headed for the wardrobe room to find another pair of sunglasses. Shelly covered her mouth to hide a giggle.

"I haven't seen Quentin in such a good mood since he got our last art director fired," Shelly confided after Jessica returned with a different pair of sunglasses. "You should steal his camera every day." Jessica had filled Shelly in on the incident, including the mysterious appearance of what

153

seemed to be a brand-new camera to replace the ruined one.

"No, thanks!" Jessica whispered back. "I've learned my lesson this time. I'm never taking anything without permission again for as long as I live . . . or at least until a very good reason comes along."

"You said you had a theory about the mysterious replacement camera," Shelly said. "Did you recognize the handwriting on the note?"

"No, it was block-printed," Jessica replied. "But I think I know who must have done it. The note is on really heavy, textured stationery. The classy, expensive kind. I know only one person who can afford stuff like that."

"Your friend Lila?" Shelly whispered.

Jessica shrugged. "It's *got* to be Lila," she said. "She must have taken pity on me at the last minute and bought a new camera just like the old one. Or she's planning to charge me outrageous interest on the loan—once I'm a rich, famous model."

"I thought she absolutely refused to lend you the money."

"She did," Jessica admitted. "But you have to understand Lila. She hates it when people think she's a pushover. She's afraid they'll ask her for money all the time if they hear she's a soft touch."

"So she did it in secret to save her reputation for being selfish and unbending?" Shelly asked, eyebrows raised in a skeptical frown.

"Exactly," Jessica agreed.

"Isn't that a little weird?"

"Like I said, you have to understand Lila."

"Jessica, if you're finished socializing over there, I want to try this with sandals on," Simone interrupted from beneath the lights. "There's a scarlet pair of Bartuccis in the wardrobe room, with high heels."

"Nobody wears high-heeled sandals with a bathing suit!" Jessica protested.

"That shows how much you know about fashion," Simone said, tilting up her nose. "Get me those sandals. *Now!*"

After shifting her position so that Shelly's back hid her from Simone, Jessica stuck out her tongue at the model.

"While Jessica gets those sandals, Shelly, give Todd a touch-up. I'm getting some shine on his face."

"Probably from Simone rubbing up against him," Jessica whispered to Shelly as she walked by on her way to the wardrobe room. She refused to run this time. She wasn't going to act as if chasing down Simone's every whim was important to her. Once inside the cluttered room she rooted around until she found a pair of red Bartucci sandals. Then she sauntered back to Simone and deposited them at her feet.

"I said *scarlet!*" Simone complained. "Those are *crimson*. Can't you do anything right?"

"Well, sor-*ry*," Jessica told Simone. Quentin was out of the room, looking for a different lens. So Jessica allowed just the right amount of cold condescension to creep into her voice and expression. *Perfect,* she thought. *Lila would be proud of me.* For an instant Simone had looked genuinely flustered.

"The scarlet sandals are behind your dressing screen," an assistant art director told Simone. From the expression on Simone's face Jessica realized the model had known it all the time. Simone fixed a bored, expectant gaze on Jessica's face. Jessica sighed and sauntered to the corner to get the scarlet sandals.

"You're going to put them on for me, aren't you?" Simone asked when Jessica dropped them at her feet.

"Oh, I forgot," Jessica said. "You haven't learned buckles yet. That's one of those advanced motor skills."

Simone began sputtering like a broken fountain. Before she could formulate a reply, Jessica felt a tug on her shoulder and whirled to see Todd standing there, his face full of dismay. "Can I talk to you a minute, Jess?" he asked, pulling her aside. Jessica was glad to leave Simone's company.

She had to admit that she'd never seen Todd looking better. His bronze shoulders, muscular arms, and lean, basketball player's build were set off to perfection by the designer swim trunks. And Michael had used a huge handful of mousse to make his hair look windblown and natural. *Too bad he's still the same old clueless Todd,* she thought.

"If you're going to start giving me orders too now that you're a hotshot fashion model," Jessica threatened, "I will personally tell Simone about the time in sixth grade when you cooked a southern meal for social studies and put in too much hot sauce and used salt instead of sugar and the whole class got sick!"

"I swear I won't give you any orders!" Todd said quickly. "But why are you being so mean to Simone?"

"In case you haven't noticed, she's the one who's treating me like dirt," Jessica pointed out.

"You're an intern. It's your job to run and get things for her."

"Jessica Wakefield is *nobody's* slave!" Jessica declared, arms folded across her chest. "But I bet you'd jump if the Fashion Witch gave *you* an order. It's really disgusting, the way you two are hanging all over each other. In case you've forgotten, you have a girlfriend!"

"Simone and I are not hanging all over each other!" Todd insisted. "It's called modeling, Jessica. I wouldn't expect you to understand, since you're only a photographer's assistant."

"What about Elizabeth? Remember her? Do you think my sister would understand?"

Todd bit his lip. "You're not going to tell her some exaggerated version of what's going on here, are you?"

"*Exaggerated?*" Jessica asked. "Why would I have to exaggerate? You're wearing a bathing suit and playing contact sports in the sand with a half-naked supermodel. In front of a roomful of witnesses! I couldn't *invent* anything better than this."

"All right, people!" Quentin called, striding back into the room. "Places, everyone! Simone and Todd, I'll want a few more shots in these suits. Then get into your second change of clothes."

Todd stepped off the set a while later so that Shelly could touch up his makeup. But he couldn't keep his eyes off Simone, posing again in the skimpy white bikini from the day before. He'd always thought he was attracted to wholesome, all-American types, like Elizabeth. But one look at Simone made his temperature shoot up, even without the bright lights.

"It's past three-thirty, but we've got several hours of work to finish here tonight," Quentin said when he stopped to switch cameras. "Can everyone stay late?"

The staff agreed immediately—even Jessica, though she rolled her eyes at Shelly as she told Quentin yes. Todd hesitated. He and Elizabeth had a date to go to Guido's after work. Jessica glared at him expectantly, but Todd avoided looking at her.

"Todd, is that OK with you?" Quentin asked. "Is there a problem?"

For a moment Todd wondered if it *would* be a problem. When he'd called Elizabeth to tell her he'd quit Varitronics and was on his way to the studio, she had seemed surprised but no longer angry. He thought she'd adjusted to the idea of him becoming a model. But she'd also said she was looking forward to their date.

"There's no problem, Quentin," Todd said. "I . . . uh . . . had some plans. But it's nothing I can't cancel."

Jessica cast him one of those witheringly cold stares she must have learned from Lila. But Todd told himself that Elizabeth would understand his decision. Elizabeth was the one who'd lectured him on the importance of making a good impression in an internship. She'd been talking all week about making sacrifices in order to build a career. Now he knew she'd been right all along.

"The brim on this hat is too wide," Simone complained during the next break from shooting. She snatched a white canvas hat from her head and threw it in Jessica's face. "Get me the other white one."

"*Flair*'s fashion experts say wide brims are chic," Jessica objected. "Besides, this is a Bartucci design. Isn't that what we're supposed to be show-casing?"

"It's casting shadows on my face," Simone explained, pronouncing every syllable distinctly, as if she were speaking to a five-year-old. "Nobody can see what I look like."

"So?" Jessica whispered. "You wouldn't want the plastic surgery scars to show, would you?" She pitched her voice loud enough for Simone to hear but too low to reach Quentin's ears. Luckily he was far across the room.

Jessica heard gasps from both Shelly and Todd when they realized what she'd said. But she kept her eyes on Simone, challenging the tall, skinny girl to respond. The stony look on the model's face made Jessica wonder if this time she'd gone too far. She dismissed the thought almost immediately. The fashion business was no place for wimps. Besides, a thrill raced through her entire body every time she saw the Toothpick at a loss for words, as she was now.

Jessica smiled sweetly. "I'll go find you that other hat," she promised.

Jessica saw the hat in the wardrobe room almost immediately. But she decided Simone could wait while she tried on a few others in front of the mirror, practicing for her own career as a model. She was sure she'd be more successful than Simone. She had more sex appeal than Simone, easily. The only thing she didn't have was Simone's height, but she knew she could overcome a tiny little obstacle like that.

"Now that Quentin doesn't hate me," she whispered to her reflection as she tied a scarf loosely around her neck, "I'll convince him to fall in love with me in no time. And my professional-looking photos are due here tomorrow." She tossed the ends of the scarf over her shoulder. "After that the sky's the limit!"

"Jessica!" called Simone's voice, managing to sound bored and exasperated at the same time. "Where is my hat?"

"I see it!" Jessica called back, hastily untying the scarf. "There's so much stuff in here, it's hard to find anything."

She tossed the hat on her head and sauntered out of the wardrobe room, hips first, in a close impersonation of Simone's sultry walk. Simone was standing near Shelly's makeup table while Quentin and Michael fussed with Todd's hair on the other side of the set. Jessica approached the tall, leggy girl and was about to whip off the hat and hand it to her.

Suddenly the tile floor slammed up to meet her. Quentin, Michael, and Todd spun around just in time to see her sprawl forward on her stomach, desperately trying to break her fall with her hands. She was sure she heard laughter coming from that side of the room.

Jessica was the only one who noticed the

movement of Simone's long, skinny foot as the model wrenched it out of the way. The Toothpick had *tripped* her!

Jessica ignored the crushing pain in her chest. She rose from the floor with all the dignity she could muster, her eyes fixed on Simone's face. *This is war,* she promised the model silently. *And Jessica Wakefield always wins.*

Chapter 11

Wednesday afternoon Elizabeth waited for the elevator on the eighth floor. She'd just come from the advertising department, where she'd been running an errand for Leona. Normally she would be thrilled to handle any detail for the managing editor. Now she just wanted the day to be over. But her watch said it was only four o'clock.

The rational part of her brain told her not to be discouraged about one rejected idea. Writers had to learn to live with rejection. But her creative mind could still visualize her "Free Style" column as a page in the magazine, with a trendy logo and a snapshot of the reader who'd submitted that month's manuscript. She could see it so clearly. Why couldn't Leona?

She stepped into the elevator and reached up to press the button for the editorial offices. On the spur of the moment she decided to visit the photo studio instead. Todd was there, working on his first real shoot. Maybe seeing him and thinking about their date that night would cheer her up. She needed something to dispel the feeling of impending doom that seemed to have settled in around her, making the elevator seem much smaller than usual.

"I have to get a grip on myself!" She said it aloud, without meaning to, and was grateful to be alone in the elevator. One failed idea didn't translate into a doomed career. It didn't mean she had no talent and would never be successful. Leona certainly hadn't treated her any differently since rejecting her idea.

She pushed open the door of the studio and was immediately sorry she'd stopped by. Todd was lying on a beach chair on the same sand-covered set Quentin had posed him on last time. But now he was wearing a swimsuit—a tight, tiny, green one that in Elizabeth's mind gave new meaning to the word *brief.* Elizabeth recognized it as an Italian design. But if one of their friends had shown up on the beach in something like that, Todd would have been the first one to make fun of it. She had to admit that he looked terrific—in an obvious sort of way. But it made her uncomfortable to see her boyfriend in such a skimpy bathing suit. And she was surprised that Todd seemed so much at ease.

Maybe I don't know Todd as well as I thought I did, she mused, hoping her face wasn't as pink as it felt.

Even worse was Simone. She was standing by Todd's beach chair, leaning over him so that her swimsuit top was practically in his face. She wore a yellow polka-dotted bikini that was nearly as skimpy as the white macramé one she'd worn the day before. And Todd was watching her so closely that he didn't even look up when Elizabeth walked into the room.

"Great, kids!" Quentin called. He sounded much happier than he had the day before. "Now I want you both standing. . . . Jess, would you move the beach chair out of the way?" Jessica complied, with a smile for Quentin and an icy gaze for Simone and Todd. "Todd, you face me, straight on," Quentin instructed. "And Simone, I want you in profile. Put your hands on Todd's shoulder and lean in to give him a kiss on the cheek, kicking up one leg behind you. . . . Perfect!"

"How about one with me kissing him on the lips?" Simone asked. "Just like this . . ." She demonstrated, and Quentin obligingly kept clicking off shots while Elizabeth felt a volcano of fury rising inside her, threatening to explode.

"Fantastic!" Quentin shouted. "Let's break now. Shelly, I think Simone's face needs a little work."

Elizabeth almost offered to work it over for her, but she fought the urge. "Todd, can I talk to you a minute?" she asked, forcing herself to stride purposefully across the room, as if to stake her claim.

"Hi, Liz!" Todd called, seeing her there for the first time. Suddenly his face colored. "Uh, um, let me get a robe." He ducked behind a screen in the corner and came out tying a terry-cloth robe around his waist. Elizabeth was sure she saw a triumphant little smile playing around the corners of Simone's usually sulky mouth.

Elizabeth leaned toward Todd for her usual peck on the lips, but he didn't seem to notice. "Elizabeth, you wouldn't believe what a great time I'm having," he said. Elizabeth tried to steer him out of Simone's earshot, but he didn't take the hint. "I mean, modeling is a lot of work too. But Quentin says I'm a natural."

Elizabeth had been hoping Todd would hate his first afternoon as a real model. She swallowed her disappointment and gave him a weak smile. "That's great, Todd. I'm glad you found something more fun than filing and photocopying."

"There is *no* comparison!" Todd raved. "I think I might have just found myself a whole new career!"

Elizabeth's now familiar sensation of impending doom pressed down harder from all sides. "But Todd," she began carefully, "the internships end a week from Friday. After that it's back to school as usual."

"I've been thinking about that," Todd said. "And if Quentin's right and I really have a future as a model, then there's no use waiting. You've been telling me all week about making sacrifices and taking risks in order to jump-start a career. I've decided that you're right."

"What are you saying?" Elizabeth asked, her eyes growing wide.

"If Quentin thinks I can make a go of it, I just might find myself an agency and start modeling right now. I'm sure I can fit in school around the edges somewhere. Simone said she could give me some tips on that. And college can wait a few years."

"Are you *crazy?*" she asked, her voice rising. She tried not to think about when he might have had time to talk with Simone about careers and education. "Your parents will never go for that!"

"I think they might, as long as I can get my high-school diploma on time," Todd countered. He glanced around at Jessica, Shelly, and Simone, who were all pretending to go about their own business while they listened to every word. "But we can talk about this later, Liz."

Elizabeth nodded, shaken. "We really do need to talk," she said. "I can't tell you how much I'm looking forward to our date tonight—"

"About that date," Todd began. "Can I get a rain check? Quentin needs me to stay late to finish this shoot."

"You're canceling our date?" Elizabeth asked in a small, desolate voice. She was terrified she would burst into tears in front of everyone. Again a smug smile tilted the corners of Simone's bloodred lips.

"You know how it is," Todd said with the dazzling grin he always used when he wanted something. "When the boss asks you to stay late, you've got to make a good impression. If I don't show that I'm willing to go the extra mile, Quentin might decide I'm not dedicated enough to want to help me get started." Suddenly his face was dead serious. "It's kind of like what you were saying about Leona the other night."

Leona didn't lure me into her office with a half-naked member of the opposite sex, Elizabeth wanted to point out. *When I'm working late, I don't have a gorgeous model kissing me.* But she wasn't about to let Simone see that she was angry at Todd—and terrified of losing him to her. "Of course," Elizabeth said in a controlled voice. "I wouldn't want to stand in your way."

She spun around and stomped out of the room. Jessica caught up with her near the elevators.

"Liz, I'm really sorry about that man-eating toothpick," Jessica said. "I promise you, I'm going to find a way to put her in her place before I'm through here."

"I hope you do," Elizabeth seethed, clenching

her hands into fists. "Did you hear the way she suggested kissing him on the lips? She knew exactly what she was doing. And she knew exactly who was watching her do it."

"Look, I've got to stay late tonight too," Jessica said. "If you're not riding with Todd, how will we both get home? Are you working late?"

"No, I'm leaving just as soon as I can," Elizabeth replied.

"You're not going home to mope in your room because you don't have a date, are you?" Jessica asked.

"No!" Elizabeth answered hotly. "I'm going home to mope in my room because Leona didn't like my brilliant idea today, and because Todd wants to destroy his life to become a model, and because you-know-who is a total witch!" She took a deep breath. "And because I don't have a date."

Jessica shook her head. "You're going about this all wrong," she said. "If a guy is treating you rotten, the best defense is a strong offense. Find somebody else to go out with here in the big city. Have a blast without Todd."

"You're absolutely right!" Elizabeth exclaimed. Suddenly she knew just what she would do with her evening.

Jessica's mouth dropped open. "I am?" she asked.

"I *refuse* to go home and feel sorry for myself,"

Elizabeth said. "I'm going right upstairs to call Enid and Maria."

"That's not precisely what I had in mind," Jessica said.

"I know, but I've been a jerk to both of them this week. This is my chance to make it up to them," Elizabeth explained. "I'll ask them to meet me here in the city. We'll go out somewhere nearby, and then I can swing back around in the Jeep and pick you up after your shoot. When will you be finished? Is eight o'clock late enough?"

"This is it!" Maria exclaimed to Enid as the two girls reached the entrance of the Mode building that evening.

"Finally!" Enid said. "After two buses and three traffic jams to get here, Liz owes us some spectacular cappuccinos. No, *double* cappuccinos. This outing would've been a lot easier if one of us had access to a car today."

"You know it, girl," Maria agreed. "If it were for anyone but Liz . . ."

"I am really glad she called tonight," Enid said. "She's been so preoccupied this week. The three of us will have a nice long chat, and we'll all feel a lot better. Besides, it feels so elegant and sophisticated, meeting in the city for coffee. Though I guess it's the kind of thing you're used to, being a former movie star."

Maria laughed as she pushed the button outside the gleaming elevator doors. "I was just a kid. I was more into cookies than cappuccino," she said. She licked her lips. "*Mmmm*, cookies. Do you think the coffee bar Liz has in mind will sell cookies too?"

"If I know Liz, the place will be flowing with chocolate chips," Enid replied.

"And she's offered to drive us home afterward in the Twinmobile," Maria said.

Enid laughed. "Thank goodness for that Jeep!" she agreed. "I couldn't face two bus rides back to Sweet Valley tonight."

The elevator opened. The girls stepped inside into the midst of a group of blatantly fashionable women. They wore stylishly long blazers and stylishly short skirts in various colors and fabrics. And almost every one of them had some variation on Elizabeth's new haircut. *It's exactly like a uniform,* Maria decided. Like everyone else, she stood facing the mirrored doors. The women stood behind her, but Maria could watch them in the mirror. And their identical, condescending expressions made them seem like clones.

"Oops, we're going to the parking garage!" Maria sang out as she felt the elevator moving downward. "We must have zoned out. We should have checked to see if the arrow was pointing up."

The women studiously avoided glancing at her and Enid, but Maria felt a wave of disapproval. Apparently talking glibly in an elevator filled with stylish snobs was a *Flair* faux pas. Maria grinned mischievously at Enid. Enid looked embarrassed.

The elevator stopped at the parking garage, and the women glided out. *Like identical suitcases on a conveyor belt,* Maria thought. As soon as the doors closed again the girls glanced at each other, and both burst into giggles.

"Send in the clones!" Maria sang.

"Did you see the one with the maroon hair?" Enid asked when she stopped laughing. "Nobody's hair is naturally that color."

"She acted like we weren't even there," Maria replied. "So did all her stuck-up friends. I bet they were holding their breath so they wouldn't breathe air that was contaminated by us, the Great Unfashionables."

"You're not unfashionable!" Enid protested. She tugged playfully on Maria's antique lace vest. "That vintage look is terrific on you. I wish I was tall enough to wear it without feeling like a kid playing dress-up."

"But you have a real sense of style," Maria argued. "I adore that scarf, by the way. At least you look professional, coming straight from work at the literary agency."

"*Professional,* maybe," Enid said. "*Stylish,* no. I

can see why Liz was afraid of looking frumpy."

"Me too," Maria agreed. "But I still think she went overboard on the new clothes."

The elevator stopped on the eleventh floor, and the girls followed Elizabeth's directions to her office. As they rounded the corner Elizabeth herself was standing in the hallway.

"Hi, guys!" Elizabeth exclaimed. Her forehead was creased, and her eyes were tired. But she seemed genuinely happy to see them. "We can get going right away. Come see my office, and I'll grab my purse."

As the girls walked back toward the elevator a few minutes later a tall woman in her late twenties hurried out of an office. "Elizabeth!" she called. "I know it's time for you to get out of here, but I was hoping you wouldn't mind staying a couple hours late. I have some ideas for upcoming articles I wanted to bounce off you."

"Leona, there's a call for you on line three!" said a receptionist who sat nearby.

"Excuse me a minute, Elizabeth," Leona said, already rushing back to her office. "This won't take long."

"So that's the famous Leona," Maria said.

"Isn't she impressive?" Elizabeth asked, pulling them into a quiet corner. "I'm sorry about tonight, you two, but—"

"What?" Enid asked. "You can't mean you're staying with her!"

173

Elizabeth seemed surprised. "I was looking forward to our evening too! But you heard Leona. She needs me here."

"Tell her you've got plans," Maria suggested. "What's the big deal?"

"I guess she would understand," Elizabeth said. "But I need to show her I'm a loyal, dedicated employee."

"You're an intern," Enid reminded her. "You don't even get *paid* for this. Besides, we both left work early and sat on two gross, smelly buses—just to spend the evening with you! What about loyalty and dedication to your friends?"

"I'm sorry," Elizabeth replied. "But I can't afford to miss this opportunity. I promise I'll make it up to you sometime soon."

"Elizabeth, I'm ready for you now!" came Leona's voice from her office.

Elizabeth shrugged and scurried to the door. After she closed it behind her, Maria turned to Enid with a sigh. "So that's life in the real world," she said sarcastically. "Looks like it's just you and me for double cappuccino."

"And a double bus ride home," Enid added. "I can't believe she stood us up."

"I hope Liz is scoring big points as a worker bee this week," Maria said as they trudged back to the elevator. "Because she sure isn't scoring any as a friend."

❖   ❖   ❖

That night Jessica waited in the wardrobe room, drinking one of Simone's bottled mineral waters and pretending to be busy. Supposedly she was organizing the Bartucci swimwear and accessories that Simone and Todd had used in the shoot. But what she was really doing was waiting for Simone and Todd to leave. She could hear the two of them in the studio, talking and laughing as they pulled on their shoes and collected their things. Todd apparently had overcome his initial awkwardness around the leggy model. She could hear him out there, dropping casual mentions of his BMW and parties at the country club.

Jessica rolled her eyes. Guys were disgusting. They'd do or say anything to impress a pretty girl.

She was glad when she heard their voices trail off as they walked out of the studio. To give them time to get out of the building, she stopped to check her appearance in the mirror, brushed her hair, and freshened her lipstick. Then she took a deep breath and sauntered to the darkroom, where Quentin was making some prints.

She opened the outer door of the darkroom and stepped into the closetlike space. The small entryway ensured complete darkness in Quentin's sanctuary. Letting any light in would destroy the pictures he was developing, and Jessica couldn't afford to have him mad at her again. She closed the outer door behind her and waited a few seconds for her eyes to adjust to the dark.

Jessica gently opened the interior door and slid soundlessly into the darkroom. The air smelled strongly of chemicals. Cutting-edge rock music spilled from a radio in the corner, filling it with sound. A dim, red safelight enabled Quentin to work but protected the prints he was making. By its eerie glow Jessica could see him standing at a long table. His back was to her, and he faced a row of tubs filled with mysterious chemicals. As Jessica watched, Quentin used tongs to carefully lift a print from the last tub. He shook it gently, spraying drops of liquid on the table. Then he hung it on some sort of clothesline that was stretched over the table.

Jessica stepped up behind him and reached around his arm to flick off the dim red light. The room was in total blackness.

Before Quentin had time to react, she wrapped her arms around him and brushed his lips with hers. "I thought you'd left," he murmured. He pulled her closer and began to kiss her, first tentatively and then with passion. Suddenly he pulled away. "You're not Simone!" he whispered, startled. Jessica leaned against his strong, broad chest and shook her head just enough for him to feel it. Then she raised her face to his once more in the dark. And he kissed her again.

Well, he's not the best kisser in the world, Jessica decided. But he wasn't bad either. In fact, she was beginning to feel herself swept away by a familiar rush of emotion. But she pulled her mind back to her goal. She had a plan to follow. And it depended on leaving Quentin wanting more. The next day she would show him the pictures Lila had taken of her on the beach. She wanted Quentin primed to give them—and her—a good, long look.

Without a word she pulled away from Quentin and hurried from the darkroom.

Unfortunately she ran into Simone as she passed through the studio on her way out.

"I thought you'd left," Jessica said, realizing as she spoke that it was the same thing Quentin had said in the darkroom.

"I did," Simone said in a smug voice. She held up a ring of keys. "But I forgot the keys to my Porsche."

Naturally Simone would drive a Porsche, Jessica thought. *Typical.*

"I saw you go into the darkroom a few minutes ago," Simone said, raising her eyebrows. "And I think I know why."

Jessica shrugged. "I just wanted to see what might develop!"

"I can guess exactly how it ended," Simone said. "If Quentin had shown the least bit of interest, you would have been in there a lot longer."

"Oh, you think so, do you?" Jessica asked mysteriously, trying not to give anything away.

"What a pathetic attempt to get Quentin's attention!" Simone said. "You can just forget it, Jessica. Quentin is *mine*. Besides, do you honestly think he'd waste his time on a *high-school* girl?"

"You seem to be taking some interest in a high-school *boy*," Jessica retorted. "And he happens to be my sister's boyfriend."

"It really *is* a shame," Simone said. "When I first saw Todd, I was hoping he was *your* boyfriend. It would have been such a pleasure to watch you squirm while I made him forget you ever existed. But obviously Todd has better taste than that."

"He *used* to," Jessica said. "I guess he's made an exception in your case. Do you think Quentin's too stupid to see that you're after Todd? And sooner or later Todd is going to hear that you're dating Quentin."

"Who ever said one guy was enough?" Simone asked with a designer shrug. "I guess that's hard for you to understand since you can't *get* even one. Anytime you need some tips on how to attract a man, just stop by, Jessica. I'd be happy to give you some expert advice."

"I'll keep that in mind," Jessica said with an innocent smile. As she watched Simone saunter out of the studio Jessica's smile turned victorious. Her mind replayed the scene in the darkroom. Simone would have a fit if she knew what was probably going on in Quentin's mind right now. By the end of the week Quentin and Jessica would be an item.

"I've got her!" Jessica said under her breath. Simone was about to be struck by Hurricane Jessica. And she was too stupid even to hear the storm warnings.

Chapter 12

Jessica raced to the mail room late Thursday morning to see if her photographs had arrived. She'd sent to the lab the film Lila had taken of her on the beach Tuesday night. And the prints were being delivered to her at *Flair* by courier. She couldn't wait to see how gorgeous and professional she looked.

As she ran into the room Cameron was poring over something at a desk in the corner.

"Cameron!" she yelled, louder than she meant to.

Cameron jumped. "Jessica!" he reacted, blushing furiously. He scrambled to put away whatever he was looking at.

"You don't have to drop everything else," Jessica said quickly. "I can help myself if you tell me where to look. I'm expecting a courier package this morning from a photo lab in Pasadena. It's for me, not Quentin."

"Right," Cameron said, still flustered. "From the lab in Pasadena."

"Is it here?" Jessica demanded excitedly. "Which pile should I look in?"

Cameron's shoulders slumped. "I . . . uh . . . have it right here," he confessed, gesturing at the papers he'd been poring over. "The lab only addressed the package to *Flair*, without your name. I kind of . . . um . . . had to open it up to see who to deliver it to."

"That's OK," Jessica said, jumping to his side. "I'm just dying to see those pictures. How do they look?"

"I guess I got a little carried away," Cameron said. "I didn't really have to go through every single photograph just to figure out who to route the package to. But you're so darn pretty in these. . . ."

Jessica grinned, feeling a blush spreading across her own face, though she wasn't sure why. Guys complimented her on her looks all the time. Cameron was no different than any other guy who'd been attracted to her. She grabbed a handful of prints from him. "Ooh," she exclaimed as she leafed through them. "These *are* great shots! Thank goodness for that camera I sto—" She stopped.

"What camera?"

"Uh, just a fancy camera I borrowed from a friend," Jessica lied.

Cameron pulled out a photograph that showed Jessica dancing in the sand, one arm reaching gracefully over her head. "You've got talent," he said in a wistful voice. "You're beautiful, and you have a special kind of charisma that jumps off the page."

"Really?" Jessica asked, hoping he'd say more.

Cameron blushed again. He dropped the photo as if it were on fire. Then he stared at the desk. "Too bad your insides aren't as attractive as your outsides," he said, his voice suddenly bitter.

"What's *that* supposed to mean?" she asked.

"I don't know why I thought you'd be any different," he said. "But I did. I thought you were special."

"You don't think so anymore?" Jessica asked, wondering why the mail-room clerk's opinion was suddenly so important to her.

"From the first time I met you, I told myself you weren't just another Simone," Cameron explained. "But you fooled me. You're no better than she is."

"*What?*" Jessica yelled, furious at being compared with her arch rival. "How can you say that?"

"You're interested only in people with classy titles or flashy cars or tons of money!"

"Where do you get off talking to me like that?" Jessica demanded, hands on her hips. "We've had a total of two conversations. You don't know enough about me to pass judgment!"

"It doesn't take long to figure out whether someone's genuine," Cameron countered, jumping from his chair to face her. "And you're not!"

"And you're a sanctimonious jerk!" Jessica yelled back, jabbing a finger at his chest. "You're stuck in a dead-end job, so you're jealous of people who have the potential to go higher than that!"

"You've got the potential to make it as a model, all right!" Cameron replied. Jessica could practically see sparks shooting through the air between them. "Every model I've ever met was vain, superficial, and hung up on appearances. You'll fit right in!"

Suddenly Jessica was aware of how close Cameron was standing. If they hadn't been screaming at each other, they could have been slow dancing. Without thinking about it, Jessica tilted her head back to kiss him. For a second Cameron seemed to be leaning forward. Then he scowled and turned away.

"And isn't that just like a model," he observed bitterly. "You all assume that every guy is dying to kiss you, anytime you're ready. Well, this guy isn't! I kiss when *I* choose to. And *only* when I choose to!"

Jessica felt her face grow prickly hot. She glared at him, humiliated and furious, as she gathered up her photographs. And she stalked out of the room, vowing never to speak to Cameron again.

※　　※　　※

Elizabeth swallowed as she stopped outside Leona's office door after lunch on Thursday. She wasn't sure why the managing editor wanted to see her. But after having her "Free Style" column idea rejected the day before, she was nervous—even though the brainstorming session Wednesday evening had been pleasant and productive.

"You wanted to see me?" Elizabeth asked, hesitating in the doorway. "Was there a problem with the research I did for you?"

Leona smiled. "No, there's been no problem with any of your assigned work, Liz. You've been consistently impressive. I just wanted to let you know about an upcoming event. Have a seat."

Elizabeth sat down, relieved. "What kind of event?" she asked. "Is there a meeting you'd like me to help you with?"

"No, nothing like that," Leona said. "This is an unofficial event—a party, really. Most of the key editors will be there. I hope you will be too."

"It sounds great," Elizabeth said. "I'd love the chance to get to know the other editors outside of work. When is it?"

"I thought you'd say that," Leona replied. "The party is tomorrow night. It's after hours, and it's not an actual *Flair*-sponsored gathering. So of course attendance is not mandatory."

Elizabeth leaned back in her chair, disappointed. "I'm glad to hear it's not mandatory," she said. "Normally I'd be excited about something like this. But I can't make it. I already have plans for tomorrow."

Leona raised her eyebrows. Then realization dawned in her eyes, and she nodded. "I understand," she said. "It's Friday night. You and Todd probably have a date planned. You don't have to cancel it. Just change the venue. In fact, most staff members bring their significant others to this kind of party. Todd is welcome to join us. I'd love to meet him."

"It's—it's not Todd!" Elizabeth stammered, surprised at Leona's persistence. "I have these two best friends I've been neglecting all week. After I got home last night, I called them and made plans to go out together tomorrow."

"I can't *order* you to go to this party, Elizabeth," Leona said, her voice suddenly cold and hard. "But I strongly recommend that you call your friends back and suggest another night for your outing."

"Leona, I really can't," Elizabeth said, wondering why she felt compelled to explain. "They're already mad at me for standing them up earlier this week. I owe this to them." She didn't explain that she and Todd were barely on speaking terms.

"Maybe I'm not making myself clear," Leona said. "You asked me earlier this week how women get ahead in this field. This is what it takes. The social side of things is just as important as the quality of work you do."

"I thought you said attendance was optional," Elizabeth ventured.

"It's optional for the average employee," Leona said. "But for people who expect to move up—both at *Flair* and in the industry at large—attendance is an absolute must. It's up to you, Liz. You have to decide if you're a fast-tracker or a middle-of-the-roader."

"Do you mean that missing one party—not even a meeting, but a *party*—could hurt my career?" Elizabeth asked.

"I don't want to make this sound like a threat," Leona said. "But I strongly suggest that attending this party and similar events is in your best interests—if you're still interested in having a future with *Flair.* If you know what's good for your career, Liz., you'll cancel out on your friends and come along."

Leona seemed like a different person. Her warmth and friendliness had evaporated. A chill skated up Elizabeth's spine. For the first time she saw a glimpse of what it would be like to have Leona angry with her. It was not a pleasant thought.

"All right," Elizabeth said weakly as she walked toward the door, anxious to get away from this new, scarier Leona. "I'll see what I can do about changing my plans," she promised. "But I might have to come alone. I don't know if Todd's busy tomorrow."

She reached the door and turned back to Leona with a new idea. "Wait a minute—is this the kind of thing I could bring Maria and Enid to?"

Leona shook her head. "I'm sorry, Liz," she said. "There's no actual rule against bringing your best chums to this sort of function. But it just isn't done. Everybody brings a date. A *real* date."

Elizabeth nodded, feeling doomed. Somehow she had to find a way to make up with Todd and to put up with his new ego. And she had to find it fast. She sighed as she plodded back to her own office.

Life in the real world was a lot more complicated than she'd imagined.

By four o'clock that afternoon Jessica had managed to force Cameron out of her mind. At least she kept telling herself she wasn't still thinking about what had happened in the mail room that morning. She couldn't believe that a guy who had seemed so nice would say such awful things about her—and then humiliate her by pulling away right before they kissed. She could have sworn he wanted that kiss as much as she had.

"But I *didn't* want it," she repeated under her breath. "I'm not interested in a guy who works in the mail room!" But why wasn't he interested in *her?*

She shoved Cameron's image out of her mind and concentrated on Quentin instead. It was time to make her next move. Finally the photographer was alone. She had seen him walk into the wardrobe room a few minutes earlier.

Jessica ducked into Michael's salon to check her reflection in the mirror. She'd persuaded him to style her hair that afternoon, and it was perfect. The longer part in front was swirled around her face in dramatic waves of gold. She wore a long white blazer over a low-cut white minidress. Both pieces were trimmed in gleaming silver. And both were still spotless since she hadn't set up any photo shoots all day. With her suntan she decided she looked much better in white than pale-skinned Simone could ever hope to look.

Jessica winked at herself in mirror. Quentin wouldn't be able to resist her. Then she strolled into the wardrobe room and stood in the doorway for a moment, watching while the photographer rummaged through colorful articles of clothing.

"Hi, Quentin," she said in her brightest, most helpful photography-intern voice. "Can I help you find something?"

Quentin opened his mouth to answer, but then he stopped, staring at her as if he'd never seen her before. He took a step closer and rested his hands on her shoulders. "Jessica!" he whispered. "It was you, wasn't it?" he asked, gazing at her with those smoky gray eyes. "You're the girl who kissed me in the darkroom last night, when I was making prints."

Jessica batted her eyelashes and smiled enigmatically. She could tell from his wide eyes and ragged breathing that Quentin was intrigued. But she couldn't make it too easy for him.

"Speaking of prints," she began after a moment, "I have a few here that I wanted to show you. I never really thought about being a model before. But a friend took one look at these and told me I had a lot of potential. What do you think?"

She handed him a half dozen of her favorite shots. While she waited for Quentin to examine them, Jessica casually began folding a pile of wrinkled scarves to show that she didn't really care about his verdict. She'd originally planned to put the photographs together into a professional portfolio, but she could do that later. Today she had Quentin's attention. She couldn't risk losing it.

Quentin stopped on the photograph of her dancing on the beach—the one Cameron had liked best. He whistled. "Jessica, I am really impressed," Quentin said at last. "You're not quite tall enough for runway modeling, but we might be able to play around that for photo work. I could help you if you're interested in taking a shot at it."

"That would be awesome!" Jessica exclaimed. She modulated her voice. "I mean, I've been watching Simone and Todd all week, and I think this is something I'd really like to try. If you think I might have the talent."

"No question about it," Quentin said. "You've got talent. You're photogenic. You have a great look—wholesome but sexy. In fact, I'd love to talk to you more about this, but I'm out of time right now. Can we discuss it over dinner tomorrow night?"

Jessica was ecstatic. "That would be great!" she replied.

"I almost forgot what I came in here for," he said, gazing around the room. "There it is," he said, pointing to two scraps in her pile of scarves. "Would you hand me those pieces of gold lamé?"

Jessica picked up the shiny bits of fabric and realized she was holding a bikini. "A bathing suit?" she asked as she handed it to him.

"We're planning a fashion spread to illustrate an article on the Return of Metallics," Quentin explained, standing in the doorway. "Simone needs to try this on ahead of time."

"Oh," Jessica said softly. Quentin left, whistling, and she plopped herself down in a chair. It was too bad that he could still remember Simone's name. But another day or two would make all the difference. Jessica almost had him exactly where she wanted him. She couldn't believe how easy it had been to manipulate him.

Quentin may be a famous photographer, she told herself, *but when it comes down to it, he's just another guy. And he's just as dumb as the rest of them.*

Thursday had been an easy but interesting day

for Todd. He hadn't been in any photo shoots. Instead he'd spent the day talking to various members of Quentin's staff, learning about lights, sets, and props. In between the lessons his thoughts had been drifting back and forth all day between Elizabeth and Simone.

He knew Elizabeth was ticked off at him. And that made him ticked off at her. For some reason it was OK for her to be too wrapped up in a career to spend time with him. But it didn't seem to work both ways.

Things were much simpler with Simone. Simone understood the pressures of a career as a model. She was a professional; she knew that touching and kissing were no big deal. They were part of the job. They were nothing for Elizabeth to have a fit about—even when the person who happened to be touching and kissing him was a sexy, six-foot-tall model with a flawless body that was frequently on display for everyone to see.

The image had just begun to flow through his mind as slowly and sweetly as molasses. And suddenly Simone stepped into the room—in the flesh, so to speak. She wore another skimpy bikini, this time in some shiny gold stuff. As always she looked like a fantasy. For a moment Todd thought he'd conjured her up, like a genie from a lamp.

"Hi, Todd," she said in that throaty voice of hers. "I was just trying this bathing suit on for an upcoming shoot. What do you think? Is it too tight?"

Todd shook his head. "It looks good," he said, keeping his eyes on her face.

"You hardly looked at it," Simone chided him, giggling. She walked over and stood very near. "Come on, Todd. I'm asking you as one professional model to another. Take a good, close look at my bikini. And tell me what you think."

Jessica sat in the wardrobe room, hoping nobody would find her there. It was late in the day, and she didn't feel like working. In another twenty minutes she could go home. Until then she was content to sit in a room that contained more beautiful outfits than even Lila's closet and to pat herself on the back for her success with Quentin fifteen minutes earlier. Suddenly she stiffened. Cameron was hesitating in the doorway, holding an overnight express package. Jessica rose from her chair.

"This just arrived for your department," he said, holding out the package. "A couple of models are in the studio, but I'm supposed to give it to Quentin or one of his assistants. You're the only other person I could find."

Jessica nodded. "I can take it," she said, feeling her cheeks turning pink again. She reached out to take the package from him, and their hands touched. Electricity crackled between them, and Cameron took her hand in his. He pulled her close and wrapped his arms around her as if he never intended to let her go. Then his lips were on hers, and he was kissing her in a way that sent fountains of sparks cascading through her body.

After a long, exquisite minute he pulled his lips from hers. Jessica stared into his deep brown eyes, sure that her heart had stopped. She could barely catch her breath.

"There's more where that came from," Cameron said simply. "We're having dinner together tomorrow night." Jessica nodded mutely, still overwhelmed from the kiss. Cameron dropped the package on the chair and disappeared through the door.

Jessica stood in the center of the cluttered room. Her head was reeling. She felt too stunned to move or even think. Suddenly she looked up. The lights in the main studio had just blinked off. Cameron said the only people left in the department were two models—Simone and Todd, she guessed. They must have closed up shop and gone home, flicking off the studio lights on their way out. That left Jessica alone, but she didn't care. Cameron had just given her one of the most incredible kisses of her life.

There's more where that came from, he had said. She closed her eyes and imagined a second kiss, even better than the first. Her eyes flew open when she remembered exactly where the first kiss had come from. *The mail room.* She was falling for a cute, sexy guy who could do absolutely nothing to help her career.

Meanwhile the jerk who could help her seemed to be falling for her. But Quentin just didn't make her heart pound the way Cameron did. What was the solution? Would she really have to choose between a great guy and a fabulous career? *And now,* she realized with a start, *I've got a date with both of them for the same night!*

"What am I going to do?" she whispered to the empty room.

Elizabeth stepped out of the elevator on the ninth floor Thursday evening, hoping Todd was still in the photography studio. She had to resolve things with him. She wanted to apologize. It was more than the unofficially mandatory office party. She'd finally admitted the truth about spending so much time away from Todd in the past week: She *missed* him. It was true that he was getting a swelled head from being told all day long how handsome he was. But that was understandable. She had to trust Todd enough to assume he'd be reasonable again as soon as the novelty of the situation had worn off.

For now she just wanted to kiss and make up. She wanted her boyfriend back.

She pushed open the door to the photo studio and realized she was too late. The room was almost completely dark. Todd and everybody else must have left for the day. Of course, she remembered, there were some smaller rooms in back, off the main studio. Maybe some of them still had lights and people in them. It was worth checking out. But first she had to light her way across the big studio.

Elizabeth groped along the wall for the overhead switch. She flicked it on. The room flooded with light, and Elizabeth blinked. She gasped. Todd and Simone stood in one corner of the room—locked in a passionate embrace. And the leggy model was wearing nothing but a shiny gold bikini.

Elizabeth couldn't breathe. Todd looked stunned, like a deer caught in the Jeep's headlights. But Simone had a triumphant smirk on her face.

That's it, Elizabeth thought, her mind spinning. She'd found the source of the suffocating certainty that something terrible was waiting to pounce. Elizabeth's world crashed around her and splintered into jagged bits. She'd been afraid of choosing between her personal life and her work life. Now she no longer had any choice. She'd lost Todd. And she'd lost her chance at a career at *Flair.*

Elizabeth fled the studio, sobbing.

Will Jessica choose Cameron or Quentin? Will Elizabeth ever manage to impress Leona? And how will the twins defeat the evil supermodel? Turn the page for a sneak peek at Sweet Valley High #130, *Model Flirt*, the second book in this very fashionable three-part miniseries. Don't miss it!

It was only nine P.M., but Elizabeth was in bed, tossing and turning. The memory of Todd and Simone together kept dancing before her eyes, tormenting her. Elizabeth flipped on her side and wrapped the covers around her, trying to shake the image from her mind. Outside, rain was pouring down steadily. Usually the sound of rain soothed her, but tonight it just added to her anxiety.

Think of the ocean, she told herself. She concentrated deeply, imagining the picturesque view at Ocean Bay. She saw hot, white sand and the foamy blue-green sea. White-capped breakers crashed onto the shore, and seagulls cut arcing patterns above the waves. Then she saw Todd and Simone walking hand in hand along the shore. Simone was barefoot and carrying her sandals in one hand, but her storklike legs were so long that she was almost as tall as Todd. *I can't believe you took her to the beach,* Elizabeth irrationally told Todd in her mind. *Our beach. . . .* Pain stabbed at her heart.

Elizabeth shook her head and threw off the covers, sitting up in bed. It was no use. She couldn't sleep. She couldn't stop thinking about Todd and Simone. Sighing deeply, she reached over and turned on the lamp next to her bed. The first thing she saw was a copy of *Flair* on her nightstand. Leona had given her a stack of back issues so she could familiarize herself with the magazine, and this one featured a barely bikini-clad Simone. Elizabeth sucked in her breath, feeling assaulted by the photograph.

She picked up the magazine and examined the cover. Usually pictures of models in bathing suits offended her feminist sensibility, but this one was particularly artistic. It had clearly been shot by Quentin Berg. The photo was in black and white, with a grainy quality that gave it a dated look. Elizabeth had to admit that Simone looked good. She was perched on a white boulder, her long legs folded gracefully underneath her. Her sleek, asymmetrically-cut jet black hair provided a sharp contrast to her flawless ivory skin. Her full lips were pursed together in a pout and her eyes stared directly at the camera, pale and strangely blank. She was obviously beautiful, but she seemed empty—and cold. And she was so skinny that she looked like a starvation victim. But obviously, that's what Todd wanted. He didn't want someone with life. He wanted someone with status. Supermodel status.

Elizabeth scowled, feeling like a nobody, a nothing. She felt like her entire self had been made worthless. She could change her interests, but she couldn't change her looks. She'd never be six feet tall. She'd never look like a supermodel. Elizabeth balled her hands into fists, seething with frustration. Then she tore off the cover of the magazine, ripping it into tiny pieces. She threw the pieces on the floor, watching in satisfaction as they scattered over her cream-colored carpet.

Sliding out of bed, Elizabeth kicked at the torn-up pieces on the floor, grinding Simone into the carpet with her heel. She paced from one side of her bedroom to the other, gnashing her teeth. She stopped at the door and surveyed her room, itching with dissatisfaction. It was so impeccably neat and orderly. She looked in disgust at her perfectly clean desk with her reference books and computer, at her armoire with her shoes all perfectly lined up, at the immaculate bookshelves. . . . Her room used to give her a sense of peace and a desire to work. Now she felt caged in. Elizabeth yanked open a window, letting in a gust of cold, windy air. Then she grabbed her clothes from the bed and threw them on the floor in a heap.

Maybe it's all my fault, Elizabeth thought, kicking her clothes out of the way as she crossed the room again. After all, she *had* been neglecting Todd. Ever since she had found out about her internship, the job had been the only thing on her mind. Todd had called her—and faxed her—and had even driven all the way to L.A. to see her. But she hadn't given him a second of her time.

Then Elizabeth dismissed the thought as ridiculous. When Todd had trained like a madman for the basketball finals last season, she had barely seen him at all. And she had understood. Besides, this internship was just two weeks long. Just because Todd hadn't bothered looking for an interesting position was no reason Elizabeth shouldn't try to make a future for herself.

Elizabeth grabbed a woolen blanket from her bed and flopped onto her pale velvet divan dejectedly. If a little bit of neglect would make Todd turn to other girls, then he wasn't worth her time—and their relationship wasn't worth her time either. Tears came to her eyes. To think that all these years could be erased in a second—in a kiss. Todd was her constant companion, her other half. It seemed like they'd always been together. And Elizabeth had thought they'd *always* be together.

A jumble of random memories flooded into her

mind, causing her chest to constrict in pain. She saw Todd at basketball practice the week before, wearing blue cutoff sweatpants and a canary yellow T-shirt. She'd stopped by to see him after school, and he'd turned and sent her a kiss, mouthing 'I love you' in the air. She saw his brown eyes staring at her intensely at Miller's Point, a popular parking spot high above Sweet Valley. And then she saw herself and Todd together one afternoon years ago, when they had shared their first tentative kiss. . . .

Elizabeth curled her legs underneath her and wrapped her blanket around her shoulders. She didn't know how she was going to make it through the school year. Sweet Valley was full of too many memories. She reached over and picked up the framed picture of Todd on her bookshelf. He was smiling at her, and his deep brown eyes were warm and trusting. She quickly put it back, laying it face down on the shelf. *How could you throw it all away, Todd?* she thought, hot tears coming to her eyes. *How could you betray me like this? How could you betray* us *like this?*

The tears trickled down her cheeks and she jumped up, brushing them angrily away. She couldn't let herself go to pieces. After all, she still had her pride. It was bad enough that Todd had fallen in love with someone else, but he had cheated on her—at her own workplace. Elizabeth shook her head in disgust. She had thought that

Todd was different from other guys. She had thought he cared about things that really mattered. But no, as soon as a supermodel walked into the vicinity, he was history.

A flash of lightning illuminated the sky and a blast of rain shot through the open window. Shivering, Elizabeth pulled the window shut. Then she prowled across the room, feeling restless. She didn't know what to do with herself. She wanted to talk to someone. Jessica was wonderful, but she needed a friend who would truly understand her situation—like Enid. Enid always managed to make her feel better. She was levelheaded and could always give Elizabeth a sense of perspective about things.

Picking the phone up off her nightstand, she carried it to the floor and plopped down on the carpet, bringing her knees up to her chest. She punched in Enid's number and waited as the phone rang. But no one answered.

Elizabeth blinked back tears, feeling a little desperate for support. She stared at the number pad, wondering if she should call Maria. She had been giving her friends the brush-off lately, and they were probably mad at her. But then again, they were her best friends. They would understand. They would be there for her.

Without thinking about it any further, Elizabeth quickly dialed Maria's number. She twisted the phone cord around her finger as the phone rang. *Maria, please be there*, she thought.

Finally Maria picked up. "Yes?" she asked, her voice giddy. Elizabeth breathed a sigh of relief.

"Maria, it's Elizabeth," she said.

"Oh, hi, Elizabeth," Maria responded, her voice turning distinctly cold. Elizabeth winced. Then she heard giggling in the background.

"Is this a bad time?" Elizabeth asked. "Is somebody over?" She twisted the phone cord harder in her hand, cutting off the circulation in her fingers.

"Enid is staying over tonight," Maria explained, her voice distant. "We're helping each other out with stuff for our internships."

"Oh," Elizabeth said softly, hit with a pang of jealousy. Enid and Maria never used to hang out without her. "Why didn't you invite me?" she asked, trying to keep the hurt out of her voice.

"Hmm," Maria said. "Just a minute." Elizabeth could tell she had covered the receiver with her hand, but her muffled voice came through anyway. "Enid, Elizabeth wants to know why we didn't invite her over." Elizabeth heard the girls giggle. Tears welled up in her eyes again. What was going on? Was the whole world turning on her?

Enid got on the phone a moment later. "Hi, Elizabeth, it's Enid," she said.

"Hi," Elizabeth responded tentatively.

Enid's voice was cold and clipped. "In answer

to your question, we weren't aware that you'd have time to hang out with two peons like us. You've been so busy with the power players that we didn't want to disturb you."

Elizabeth didn't even have the energy to respond. She said good-bye and hung up the phone.

Elizabeth wrapped her arms around her body, feeling worse than she had before. She was completely alone in the world. First she'd lost Todd. Now she'd lost her two best friends.

The rain pelted down around her, enveloping her in her solitude.

Todd took Simone's hand and spun her around the center of the dance floor. It was almost midnight, and they were at the Edge, a hip new nightclub in downtown L.A. This was the latest he'd ever been out on a school night. The dance floor was packed with a chichi L.A. crowd, and loud techno music blasted from the speakers. Todd felt his head whirling with the pulsing beat of the electric music.

"This is what it's like living on the edge, Todd," Simone whispered in a husky voice in his ear. "How do you like it?"

Todd shrugged. "No big deal," he said, trying to sound cool. But his voice came out as a squeak and he blushed.

Simone grinned. "You are so *cute*, Todd," she

squealed. Todd's blush deepened, but Simone was already turning her attention to the other side of the room. "Look," she said, pointing an elegant finger at the bar. "That's Sven Sorensen, the editor in chief of *Ingenue* magazine."

Todd followed her gaze. A Swedish-looking man with a blond beard was sitting at the bar with a group of tall models crowded around him.

Todd nodded, searching in vain for something intelligent to say. Then he realized that Simone wasn't paying attention anyway. She was too busy posing for Sven. She steered herself and Todd around so he could get a view of her profile. "Spin me, Todd," she commanded in an intense voice. Todd swung her around obediently, and she twirled wildly, trying to get Sven's attention.

Todd blushed, feeling more self-conscious than ever. He could see every guy in the place looking at him with total envy. He was wearing jeans and a t-shirt, and he wished he'd worn something a little more hip. The crowd was made up of chic actors and models, and they were all dressed almost entirely in black. The women were all wearing short skirts and tight dresses, and most of the guys had on black jeans and funky retro jackets.

Sven stood up from the bar, and Simone stopped midspin. "Oh, I'll be right back," she said, her voice breathless. Then she rushed off.

Todd stood in the middle of the dance floor. He

tried to make out Simone through the crowd, but gyrating bodies blocked his view. There were a few couples on the dance floor, but most of the people were dancing alone, swaying to the music as if they were in a trance.

"Hey, you wanna join the Love Parade?" a sultry voice whispered in his ear.

"Huh?" Todd said, blinking. He turned to see a woman with short, scarlet hair standing by his side. She had an earring in her nose and an earring in her lip. A trail of dancers followed her in a line, bobbing rhythmically in an almost hypnotic state.

"It's a communion with Being," she said. "You close your eyes and let the music fill your body."

"C'mon, get in line," urged a blond woman with a purple streak in her hair. "You'll see. It's a natural high."

"Uh, no thanks," Todd said quickly. "I was just going to get a drink."

He waved and walked away, the eerie sound of the women's laughter echoing in his ears. Weaving through the grinding bodies, he made his way quickly to the bar.

"What'll you have?" the bartender barked. He was a bulky man with a huge grizzly beard.

Todd gulped. He was tempted to order a drink, but he was underage. If he got carded, he would get kicked out of the club and would be totally humiliated.

"Just a mineral water," he said quickly.

The bartender nodded and picked up a bottle of seltzer. He poured the bubbling water into a tall glass.

Todd picked up his drink and leaned against the bar, taking in the surroundings. The club was done in ultramodern decor, with stark white tables and shiny black floors. A flashing neon red strip surrounded the wall, and a shimmering disco ball hung over the middle of the dance floor. The stylish crowd looked as electric as the club itself.

Todd took a sip of his drink, feeling entirely out of place. He wondered if anybody knew he was underage. He was trying to play it cool, but he felt as if he was wearing a huge sign on his back that screamed *"Sixteen!"*

"Oh, Todd, there you are!" Simone breathed by his side. "C'mon, let's go back to the dance floor," she said, taking his hand.

"Sure," Todd agreed, downing his drink and following her. He definitely preferred the dance floor to the bar. Dancing was one thing he could legitimately do. At the bar, he felt like a total fraud.

Simone wrapped her arms around his waist and pressed her body to his.

Todd coughed uncomfortably, shifting back up a few inches. "So, did you have any luck with the editor in chief of *Ingenue?*" he asked.

Simone nodded in pleasure. "He's going to call

me," she said. "He wants to use me for the cover of the next issue." She giggled gleefully. "That means I'll be replacing Justine Laroche. She's going to be *green*."

"Hey, that's great," Todd said, trying to sound happy for her. *But I just can't think of a modeling job as important*, he realized. Then he swallowed hard, suddenly struck by how hypocritical he was being. *He* was a model too. This was his crowd now.

As he danced with Simone, Todd looked at the beautiful people around him and tried to convince himself that he was having a great time—and that the nagging feeling in the pit of his stomach had nothing to do with Elizabeth. He decided that he must be allergic to the shrimp cocktail he and Simone had eaten earlier.

Then, out of the corner of his eye, he glimpsed a blond girl across the dance floor. For a split second his heart leaped. *Elizabeth!* he thought, the blood pounding in his temples. Maybe she had come here to find him—to reconcile with him. But then the girl turned. It wasn't Elizabeth. Simone pulled him closer in his arms.

A wave of disappointment washed over him, and suddenly Elizabeth's bitter words came back to him. *You're not the person I thought you were.* Todd felt a sharp pang in his heart.

He shook off his negative feelings. Obviously

Elizabeth was right: he wasn't just a normal teenager. He was *model* material. He was meant for fame and fortune. It was going to be difficult to leave his old life behind, but he'd have to get used to it. He'd have to rise to the challenge.

I'm happy to be in Simone's arms, he told himself. *Very, very happy.*

Jessica paused on the top rung of a six-foot ladder in the main photography studio, surveying her work. For the past hour, she had been setting up for the morning's shoot. Nick Nolan, the set director, had come in early to prep her. It was a Greek isles scene with a bright blue backdrop, huge fake rocks, and a cascading waterfall.

Jessica gazed at the set in satisfaction. She had transformed the cool, airy studio into a hot Mediterranean paradise. The fake rocks cluttered together really looked like dusty white boulders, and they glinted against the backdrop as if against a blinding blue sky. Jessica had propped up the waterfall on the far left, but she wasn't quite sure how to hook up the mechanism.

She climbed all the way to the top of the ladder and carefully positioned the lights above the backdrop, trying to set them up just like Quentin did. Then she stepped down carefully and took a seat on the highest rung. She rubbed her shoulders and stretched out her neck. It was only ten A.M., and

Jessica's back and shoulders were already aching from moving the fake rocks around and transporting huge buckets of water.

Where is everybody? Jessica wondered. Usually Quentin was there at the crack of dawn, barking out orders. And Simone normally didn't give Jessica a moment's peace, keeping her occupied with the most mundane tasks imaginable. *Maybe she won't show up,* Jessica thought hopefully. *Maybe one of her high heels got caught in a sewage drain and she twisted her ankle. Or maybe she slipped down the drain entirely.* Then Quentin would have no choice but to use Jessica in her place. With Simone out of the way, Jessica was sure she could get through to Quentin.

The door swung open and Quentin breezed through, a camera slung over his shoulder. Jessica's tongue went dry. What if Quentin had forgotten all about the day before in the darkroom? What if he forgot about their date entirely? After all, you could never tell with artists. And Quentin was a particularly temperamental one.

But Quentin whistled under his breath as he took in the set. "Hey, looks good," he said, smiling up at her. "A Greek paradise and a Greek goddess on her modern Mount Olympus." He sauntered over to her. "Want some help getting down from there?"

"Sure," Jessica said softly, standing up and turning around.

Jessica took a few steps down the ladder. Then Quentin put strong arms around her waist and lifted her to the floor. His hands lingered on her waist as he turned her around to face him. "Looking forward to our dinner tonight?" he asked in a low voice.

"Of course," Jessica said coyly.

"You should be, because I'm taking you to the most exclusive restaurant in all of L.A.," he whispered in her ear. "It's called Chez Paul's and it's on Hollywood Boulevard. I'll meet you there at eight."

"Am I interrupting something?" came a saucy voice from behind them. Jessica and Quentin whirled around. It was Simone, a lazy catlike look of contentment on her cold features. Jessica bit her lip. It was a well-known fact at *Flair* that Simone and Quentin had been involved for some time. Jessica was thrilled to flaunt her flirtation with Quentin, but she wasn't sure he'd feel the same way.

Quentin looked disturbed. "Simone, you're late," he said flatly.

Simone shrugged. "I needed my beauty sleep."

Quentin headed for the darkroom, suddenly all business. "Simone, go to wardrobe. Jessica, set up the lights. We'll be shooting in an hour."

Jessica pounced on Simone as soon as Quentin had disappeared into his cave of chemicals. "So, did you have fun with my sister's boyfriend last night?"

Simone was totally unperturbed by Jessica's attitude. "Todd's okay for a high school boy," she responded. "He'll be good for a few photo ops, at least.

"Photo ops?" Jessica demanded. "Like what?"

Simone whipped out a copy of *Los Angeles Living* and held it up for to Jessica see. On the front page was a huge, tacky color photo of Todd in Simone's arms.

Jessica was speechless. This girl was too much. She was just glad that Elizabeth would never read a paper of such low quality. If she saw the photo, she'd really flip out.

"Now, if you'll excuse me," Simone purred, waltzing past her, "I've got to get dressed." She turned back before she entered the dressing room. "Oh, I'd like to try out a few pairs of shoes. Would you mind bringing me a half-dozen pairs of Italian sandals from wardrobe?"

Jessica's eyes narrowed as she walked away to do the Toothpick's bidding. She was going to find a way to get Simone, if it was the last thing she did.

YOU COULD WIN AN APPEARANCE IN SWEET VALLEY HIGH!

GRAND PRIZE:
Appear in a Sweet Valley High book—and win a trip to New York City to have lunch with Sweet Valley creator, Francine Pascal, and TV stars Cynthia and Brittany Daniel; a professional makeover by a *YM* magazine makeup artist; and a personally autographed collection of Sweet Valley High books

100 FIRST PRIZES:
The *Backstreet Boys'* hot new CD and cool *Backstreet Boys* merchandise

500 SECOND PRIZES:
Sweet Valley books and videos

✂

OFFICIAL ENTRY FORM

ANSWER THE FOLLOWING AND YOU COULD WIN THE GRAND PRIZE:

What is the name of the fashion magazine that Jessica and Elizabeth are interning at in Sweet Valley High #129, *Cover Girls*? (Hint: 5 letters)

Answer _____

Name _____ Birthday___/___/___

Address_____

City _____ State _____ Zip _____

Mail to: Bantam Doubleday Dell Series Marketing, Attn: SVH Sweepstakes, 1540 Broadway, 20th floor, New York, NY 10036

Bantam Books in the Sweet Valley High series
Ask your bookseller for the books you have missed

SIGN UP FOR THE
SWEET VALLEY HIGH®
FAN CLUB!

Hey, girls! Get all the gossip on Sweet
Valley High's® most popular teenagers
when you join our fantastic Fan Club!
As a member, you'll get all of this really
cool stuff:

- Membership Card with your own
  personal Fan Club ID number
- A Sweet Valley High® Secret
  Treasure Box
- Sweet Valley High® Stationery
- Official Fan Club Pencil (for secret
  note writing!)
- Three Bookmarks
- A "Members Only" Door Hanger
- Two Skeins of J. & P. Coats® Embroidery
  Floss with flower barrette instruction
  leaflet
- Two editions of *The Oracle* newsletter
- Plus exclusive Sweet Valley High®
  product offers, special savings,
  contests, and much more!

Be the first to find out what Jessica & Elizabeth Wakefield are up to by joining the
Sweet Valley High® Fan Club for the one-year membership fee of only $6.95 each
for U.S. residents, $8.25 for Canadian residents (U.S. currency). Includes shipping
& handling.

Send a check or money order (do not send cash) made payable to "Sweet Valley
High® Fan Club" along with this form to:

SWEET VALLEY HIGH® FAN CLUB, BOX 3919-B, SCHAUMBURG, IL 60168-3919

NAME_____
            (Please print clearly)

ADDRESS_____

CITY_____ STATE _____ ZIP_____
                                                        (Required)

AGE_____ BIRTHDAY_____ /_____ /_____

Offer good while supplies last. Allow 6-8 weeks after check clearance for delivery. Addresses without ZIP
codes cannot be honored. Offer good in USA & Canada only. Void where prohibited by law.
©1993 by Francine Pascal   LCI-1383-123